A LIST TO DIE FOR

GRAHAM J. BURLEM

© Graham Burlem Copyright 2017

Published by Graham Burlem

All rights reserved. No part of this book may be reproduced, adapted, stored in a retrieval system or transmitted by any means, electronic, mechanical, photocopying, or otherwise without the prior written permission of the author.

The rights of Graham Burlem to be identified as the author of this work have been asserted in accordance with the Copyright, Designs and Patents Act 1988.

This is a work of fiction. Names, characters, businesses, places, events and incidents are either the products of the author's imagination or used in a fictitious manner. Any resemblance to actual persons, living or dead, or actual events is purely coincidental.

A CIP catalogue record for this book is available from the British Library.

ISBN:1979318298

Book Layout by www.ebooksbydesign.co

PULL UP A CHAIR AND I'LL TELL YOU A TALE

List of Characters

JACK KREEGER	CASINO OWNER & FATHER OF KIDNAPPED SON.
EDDIE SUTTON	PRIVATE INVESTIGATOR
TONY KREEGER	SON THAT'S BEEN KIDNAPPED
RONNIE MILLER	JACK KREEGER'S BUSINESS PARTNER
ZOE FONTAINE	TONY'S GIRLFRIEND
STEVE	OWNER OF SNOOKER CLUB ANDEDDIE'S FRIEND
MAXINE ANDREWS	GENERAL MANAGER OF THE CASINO
ARNIEA EDDIE'S	SNOUT
RICKY HOUSTON	CROUPIER AT CASINO & TONY'S FRIEND
TOM STAFFORD	DETECTIVE CHIEF INSPECTOR
DANNY CARLIN	DRUG DEALER
COLLETTE HAMMOND	DANNY'S ENFORCER
LEON DOORELL	PIMP
DAVINA MILLER	RONNIE'S DAUGHTER
TERRYJACK'S	MINDER & CHAUFFER

CHAPTER 1

He said to be there at 4 p.m. I was. On the dot. Because you didn't keep Jack Kreeger waiting. The black electric gates closed behind me. The tyres of my Beema crunched on the driveway gravel. The sun slipped behind some clouds, things turned grey. I hoped it wasn't an omen. Someone opened the driver's door.

"Eddie, right?" I nodded. "It's Eddie, isn't it? I remember you from the jewellery shop business. The governor's waiting."

I followed him into the large red brick mansion. Terry hadn't changed much. A pound or two heavier perhaps. But still stocky with that ponytail. An earring, that was new. A small diamond stud in the left lobe, probably nicked. I followed him down a long wide highly polished parquet hall. The monotony of lime-green walls broken every so often by still life paintings, an orchard with red apples hanging from the trees, a windmill on top of a hill. He opened double doors at the end and ushered me ahead of him.

"Eddie Sutton, guv!"

The library was large; there were wall-to-wall walnut bookcases filled to the gunnels. Wilton oxblood coloured carpet deep enough to put a shine on my suede shoes. And there on the edge of a huge mahogany desk sat Jack Kreeger, oval face, silvery thinning hair, a nose like a piece of putty stuck on his face, bushy eyebrows nearly over the eyelids. He was in a navy mohair suit, blue oxford cotton shirt and maroon tie.

I wondered again what this was about. He'd been cryptic on the phone, talking for five minutes about wanting to see me but not really saying anything. But then it's an enquiry agent's lot to listen. Not only to what's being said but to what's not as well. And he'd said nothing at great length except could I call at his house off Hampstead Heath. 4 p.m. would be good. Which in Kreeger speak meant 'Be here then'. He came off his desk and offered his hand.

"Long time no see, Eddie."

"Nice to see you again, Mister Kreeger."

"Jack, please! Have a seat. How are you?"

I dropped into a leather winged armchair. All I could remember of our chat was that it was a very sensitive matter, and urgent. He sat behind his desk staring at me, drumming his fingers.

"Fine, thanks, and you?"

"Could be better."

"Oh?"

"There's a bit of a problem. And I thought you'd be the man to help because of how you handled the jewellery shop business. Mrs Kreeger and I were very impressed."

"How is she?"

He lifted a leather-bound photo holder near him and stared at it wistfully for a while. I was going to say something. But there are times when you just know to keep your gob shut.

"Mrs Kreeger passed away just under a year ago."

"I'm sorry to hear that. I only met her a couple of times. But she was always nice to me." 'A slice of my apple cake, Mister Sutton. I do all my own baking, you know. There hasn't been a shop-bought cake in this house for years.' And then she'd plonked a piece on my plate that would have given King Kong indigestion. "Very sorry to hear that, Jack."

"We were married for thirty years. I couldn't ever remember her being really ill, apart from the odd bouts of flu or a cough. Then one morning my Kitty wakes up, says she's not feeling so well and a few months later she's dead from stomach cancer."

I didn't say anything. Because what can you say?

He went back to drumming his fingers.

"I suppose you're wondering why I asked you here?"

"It crossed my mind."

"Like I said we were very happy about the business with the jeweller, which made me think of you."

He walked over to the window hands in trouser pockets and stared at the tennis court. At the white lines and the net thrown over itself just visible in the fading light, then puffed a couple of shots from an inhaler. He looked at me looking at it and said,

"Asthma. It's brought on by anxiety. What the quacks call an anxiety episode. But I'll be okay. Once I'm rid of the anxiety, that is."

I was going to ask what a multimillionaire living in a five or six million-pound house in Hampstead would have to be anxious about. But I didn't get the chance.

"There's a bit of a problem. That's why I rang you."

"What are we talking about?"

"Kidnap!"

"You want me to kidnap someone?"

He pulled a face and said,

"Do me a favour! I'm sixty-three. I'm planning on retiring soon. Not starting a career as a low life. No. It's my son, Tony. He's been kidnapped."

"Shit! How? When?"

"The early hours of this morning. In the car park of his flats."

"I can tell you right now what to do, Jack. Ring the

police." He shook his head and kept shaking it. "They're the best equipped, best experienced at dealing with this kind of thing."

I sat looking at him. There was no colour in his face. The lines on his forehead were deep, corrugated.

"That's the ex-copper in you talking, Eddie."

"No. That's common sense talking."

He buzzed his intercom.

"Lilly, we want …" He looked over and asked if I wanted tea or coffee.

"Whatever! I don't think I'm going to be here that much longer."

"Pot of coffee. Small jug of cream, and sugar."

"I'm telling you, Jack, 999 tout-suite!"

"If only it was that simple." He took another couple of puffs and a deep breath. "Cannot do, Eddie. They start putting their size fourteens over things including my life, and well, let's say I wouldn't want that. Besides, I think I know who's taken him."

"But you're talking kidnap, Jack!"

"The way I handled the jewellery shop business, for instance. It's not the first time I've used that approach. The cops will discover I don't do small claims court actions, if you get my drift. And they'll discover other things that I'd rather they didn't."

The jewellery shop business is how I'd first met Jack. He'd had a robbery at the house and wanted someone to find the missing stuff. He'd asked around and a few faces had recommended me. What had upset Kitty Kreeger most was the theft of her mother's wedding and engagement rings. 'The silver, the paintings! That's just stuff. But the rings …' and she'd become tearful. And if Kitty was upset you can bet your last euro Jack was 'upsetter' because his Kitty was. So he hired me to trace them. And I did, to an antiques and jewellers shop in Blackheath. I explained to the owner they were stolen goods. Even showed him photographs. But he wasn't having any of it. He'd bought them in good faith and if we wanted them back the price was ten grand. He was a smug little bastard. Said we could go through the appropriate channels, police, insurers, but of course they might get sold in the meantime. I told Jack. Jack told Terry to take me back there to identify the shop and the owner. Then he was to have a word with him. The conversation consisted of Terry telling me to lock the door and pull the blind down. Then before I realised what was happening, he'd shoved the shopkeeper's face into a glass-fronted wall-mounted showcase. Blood trickled over the spidery cracks. Some dripped onto the black laminate flooring, drip drop, drip drip, and then onto the owner's shoes.

The violence took me by surprise. I was expecting intimidation, maybe even a shove or two. But Terry didn't do half measures. He got hold of the owner and dragged him up the shop and dumped him in a chair. The poor bastard just sat there shaking, blood from his nose running into his mouth then onto the front of his shirt. He folded his arms and began rocking back and forth. Then his teeth began chattering as if he were freezing though it was a warm summer afternoon.

"You got two rings belonging to my governor," Terry shouted. I pointed to them sitting on the shelf of another wall cabinet. "Keys," Terry demanded. "Unless you'd like me to use your head!"

"They're in the till" were the only four words he spoke throughout.

There was a knock on Jack's door bringing me back to the present from recollections of that day. It opened. I anticipated Lilly being size eight, twenty-eight, five foot eight. I was out by eight inches and about thirty years. She was five foot, in her sixties, with grey hair scraped back so tightly it was a wonder her scalp got any circulation. She plonked a tray on his desk.

"I put some apple cake out as well."

"Thanks, Lilly!"

"Anything else, Mister Jack?"

"No."

"Enjoy."

He poured some coffee and slid it across to me.

"Help yourself to cream and sugar. And now you've met the domestic staff. Terry's my driver and minder, Lilly's my housekeeper."

"Whatever! I still say ring the cops." I stirred in some cream and sugar and took a sip. It reminded me of the coffee his Kitty made. I took a piece of apple cake. Hers had been better. "What d'you mean you know who might have taken him?"

He drank his coffee with the saucer under the cup and between short little sips said,

"I had a business partner until recently. Ronnie Miller. We'd known each other for fifty years, been in business together for twenty-five. We'd progressed from betting shops to running one of the biggest and most successful independent gambling casinos in London. The Freemont, off the Brompton Road. But you know all this from last time."

I nodded. It was for the smart set. For those with so much money and class you imagined them putting Perrier in their steam irons.

"So what's the club got to do with the kidnapping?"

"I'm coming to it." He topped up my cup. "Never mind not being here too long. Drink up. You want some fireworks in that?"

"Why not! It's nearly November."

He took a bottle of Martel from a drinks cabinet and

poured a slug in.

"So?"

"Everything's going fine. We're making millions. It's the place to go. The car park's always full. The surrounding roads are parked Roller to Roller."

"I have a feeling this story doesn't end with they all lived happily ever after."

"They do not. Because of stomach cancer."

"Mrs Kreeger. I still don't see," I replied.

He lifted a palm.

"The quacks in London couldn't help. Then we heard about a clinic in Philadelphia. So we went there. It didn't work out. So my Kitty came back to die with the family around her."

"You and Tony?"

"And Lucy, my daughter. She's a teacher in Manchester where she lives with her boyfriend, Karl, a dentist."

"I don't want to sound unkind, but …"

"I was away from the club for about six months in all. When I finally got back in the saddle, the place was like something out of Sodom and Gomorra. Ronnie had been dealing drugs. But big time, supplied by a guy named Danny Carlin and fixing up whores for clients pimped by a Leon Doorrell. Well, it couldn't go on. So I bought Ronnie out, and told Carlin and Doorrell to get lost. Then hired a few extra heavies in the guise of security to emphasise my point in case of repercussions."

"I bet Danny didn't take it too well!"

"You know him?"

"Oh, yeah! You certainly know how to pick your enemies! I still don't see …"

"Ronnie went to live in Spain. I think he might have sold out anyway in a while. He'd had enough of London and what with the cost of his divorce and everything.

Anyway, he was always fearful he knew too much and that one day someone might try and silence him. Run him over, drown him in his pool, poison his food in a restaurant." He looked me up and down and said, "Don't laugh, Eddie. The world's full of un-nice people."

I took another sip of my drink. The brandy had definitely improved the chicory.

"So Ronnie took out insurance. He kept a notebook, with a list, full of lots of juicy stuff."

"How d'you mean juicy?"

He looked as though he was deciding how far he could take me into his confidence. I must have passed muster because he said,

"Serious stuff. Incriminating. Dynamite in the right hands."

"Stuff?"

"About all the drug deals Carlin had done at the Freemont. Quantities, dates. And the people supplied. Celebs, journalists, sports people. The names of cops on his payroll to look the other way. The name of a solicitor at the CPS and the nature of the blackmail Danny had on her which he used to get her to purposely balls up a prosecution against him."

"Jesus!"

"And stuff on Doorrell. Cops on vice to develop selective amnesia. A record of A-listers he supplied whores for. The names of two DCs paid to frame a pimp for a robbery because he was trying to muscle in on Leon's territory."

"And how would Ronnie know all this stuff?"

"There are three activities that loosen people's tongues. Drinking, gambling and fucking. And he'd have been present at two of them and listening."

"You ever seen this book?" He shook his head. "So it might not even exist."

"If Ronnie said it did. It did. I was the PR man in our partnership. The schmooze. He was the fixer. He once told me he had enough shit on enough people for us never to be touched by anyone. That's why I'm sure we were never bothered at the casino with cops, Health and Safety, or protection."

"So even if it does exist, what's all this got to do with the price of fish?"

"Ronnie died just over a month ago in Du Casa where he lived. Heart attack. A legitimate one. He was in his pool. The woman he lives with dived in to help. Managed to drag him out, but … I'm one of his beneficiaries. He's left me a box of miscellaneous stuff."

And then it all fell into place. Ronnie, Kitty, the casino, the drugs, the girls. I sat back in the chair, my head supported by laced fingers and smiled.

"I knew you were bright, Eddie. Knew it from the moment I hired you to find my Kit's rings. You've got it, haven't you?"

"Yup! The book's in the box and the book's the ransom."

"In spades!"

"What if the book's not been left to you?"

"It has. He once told me if anything happened to him, he'd let me have it, because I'd know what to do with it."

"So where is it?"

"Still in Spain. Should be with a firm of City solicitors in the next few days."

"And you think it's either Danny, or this Doorrell guy that's taken your Tony?"

He finished his drink and poured himself another and held the bottle towards me.

"No thanks. I'm driving."

"My guess is at some time one of them threatened Ronnie or tried to intimidate him in some way and he told them what he had. And now he's dead they want it. And …"

"And?"

"They're the only two I know with the balls to try this."

"You sure Ronnie's death was legit?"

"Yeah! We're talking Ronnie Miller. Not Harry Lime. I spoke to his girlfriend when I heard. I was expecting some dipsy little scrubber at the other end of the phone. You know, all gloss lipstick and tits. But she's English ex-pat, sounded early forties. Very pleasant actually. There's something in the back of my mind about her having been a teacher. But I might be wrong about that. Anyway! She gave it to me chapter and verse about what happened."

He was right about Danny Carlin having the balls for it. A property developer whose real money came from dealing. And I don't mean flats and houses.

"Who's this Doorrell guy?"

"A very rich pimp. He runs high-class girls from places like mine."

Dusk had turned to early evening. Tiny yellow lights came on in the trees behind the tennis court, and a spotlight played on a fountain beside it gushing blue- and pink- and orange-coloured water.

I sat there looking at him. All that money. All that power and now over a barrel from a problem not of his making. And then it occurred to me to ask why I was there.

"I want you to find my Tony and bring him back."

"Yeah, right!"

"Why d'you think I called you! Just to tell you my tale of woe?"

"Me? Not me, Jack! Get Terry, your minder."

"Terry? If you want to intimidate someone, or beat the shit out of them, Terry's your man. But this is going to take savvy."

"Fix up a swap and go there six-handed with shooters."

He was shaking his head before I'd even finished the sentence.

"Tony has to be recovered without me surrendering the book."

"Why?"

"It incriminates me by association with Ronnie. And by a couple of other things I got up to that's sure to be in there. It leaves me open to blackmail and prosecution."

"What things? You haven't killed anyone, have you?"

"Do me a favour!

"What things, Jack?"

He hesitated for a while then said,

"Arranging for the breaking of some people's legs from time to time. Just to let them know we don't allow cheating at the tables. Bribing a council official to pass a property development planning application or two." He shrugged. "That sort of thing. Nothing really, really serious."

"On second thoughts, I think I will have that drink."

I mulled things over as he poured me another. He was right. He couldn't go to the police. And he couldn't surrender the book. But I wasn't the man for this job.

"I deliver summons, Jack. Follow people. I can even do a bit of classy breaking and entering when necessary. But finding kidnapped people? Sorry. Not in my job description."

"You're halfway there, knowing who the likely kidnappers are. My bequest is going to be with solicitors in the next seventy-two hours or so. Four, five days, it's all over."

"I don't think so. I'll have a word with a pal of mine. Perhaps between us we can come up with a face whose alley this is up."

"No. I want you. You're sharp Eddie. You've got contacts. You know your way around. If anyone's going to do it, it's you."

"Sorry, Jack!"

"I'll pay you ten grand up front. And another fifteen when Tony's back."

It did make me think twice. And then he said cash. And that made me think a third time. Not that money's my be-all and end-all. I like money. Especially as I was brought up on a council estate in Clapton, North East London, with very little of it around. I like what it buys. Good clothes, eating in good restaurants, my new Beema. There's something nice and warm and reassuring about having money. It's like a third parent looking out for you. Though I don't let it go to my head. It says in the Bible you should give to the poor, which is right. But it doesn't say you should be one of them.

"Twenty-five grand!" I exclaimed.

"Yes."

"In cash?"

"Yes. Sounds like you're up for it after all."

Jack took a white A4 envelope from a drawer and dropped it on his desk.

"Want to count it?"

"You've got an honest face."

"So, we're on?"

"I guess so," I replied, putting it in my pocket.

"Where do we start?"

"At the beginning."

The beginning was telling me Tony worked at the casino as a pit boss, and was dating a croupier named Zoe. They'd come back at about 4a.m. to his place. Were walking from the car park when three guys jumped out of a van, shoved her over, grabbed Tony, put a hood over his head, bundled him into the van and took off.

"Anyone contacted you yet?"

"This morning. They used some electronic device to distort the sound. But they said the ransom was Miller's book. I told them I didn't have it. That I'd be getting it in a few days. They said to put an ad in the *Times* Personal column when I did. 'Mr & Mrs Freemont of SW3 announce the safe arrival of a baby son named Ronnie.' And then I'd be contacted with instructions."

"This girl, Zoe. How long's she been working for you?"

"Why? You think she may have something to do with it?"

"Wooo! Don't let's jump the gun, Jack."

"I've told him a million times not to get involved with the croupiers. But does he take notice? No. Just goes on banging them left, right and centre. One after another. I might as well talk to the pavements for all the notice he takes. For all the notice he takes about anything I say, come to think of it."

"What about other friends?"

"Mike Lane. Nice kid. I play poker with his father. They've known each other since they were teenagers. And Ricky Houston, a croupier at the club. They seem quite chummy. Why d'you want to know about his friends?"

"Just building a picture. Anyone else?"

"Davina, Ronnie's daughter. They're close. We once hoped that they might get together romantically."

"And?"

He shook his head.

"Never happened!"

"Talking of pictures. D'you have one of Tony?"

He handed me another photo holder. Tony was slim, in his late twenties. He had dark curly hair. Dark eyes set in an oval face. His father's nose, Kitty's smile. He was in a white T-shirt and jeans and sat with hands on knees on the stone steps of a church.

"It was taken on holiday this year. So it's recent."

There were several other photos on his desk. One of

Jack beside a man his age, his size. Grey hair. Not a single strand of black, cut short, almost crew cut. Shadows under small eyes. Prominent nose. The skin taut, unrealistically unlined for someone his age, telling you he'd had cosmetic surgery. The pair in evening suits side by side smiling. They might have been brothers. But they were just business partners.

"And that's Ronnie, I presume?" He nodded.

"Anything else?"

"Tony's address, Zoe's and this Ricky's as well, and their phone numbers. Arrange membership for me at the Freemont, so that I can come and go without a fuss. If anybody asks, I'm advising about improved security."

"Anything else?"

"And Davina's details. Who knows about the snatch?"

"Terry and Max."

"Max?"

"Max Andrews. My general manager at the Freemont."

"Can you trust him?"

"Her. Sorry. Maxine. Yes."

"Maybe I'll meet with her to arrange a cover story for Tony's absence."

He came around the desk and stood over me.

"This will turn out okay, won't it, Eddie?"

"I'll do my very best, Jack. But like I said, kidnap's not my best game."

He took a double puff on the inhaler.

"Fucking bastards!" he cursed. "If I get my hands on who did it … I know people who for a few grand will …"

"Stop right there! I don't want to know. Anyone turns up floating in Millwall dock, I don't need the law knocking on my door. I'll come back later, if that's okay, with some telephone recording equipment."

"Sure."

"That's it for now then."

He leaned over his desk and buzzed a different intercom and Terry appeared.

"Show Eddie to his car, Terry."

"See you later, Jack" and as I left I noticed he'd gone back to staring at the photo of Kitty.

CHAPTER 2

Jack phoned me with the addresses and phone numbers I needed while I was driving home. Zoe lived in Greencroft Gardens off Finchley Road, which I was almost passing. So I decided to take a chance and see if she was in.

The houses were all late Victorian, red brick, four and five storeys with square bay windows. Nearly all converted into self-contained flats. Hers was halfway down. First floor, a one-bedder.

She answered on the second buzz. She had a smooth mellow voice that sounded as though elocution hadn't quite knocked the Essex out of it. But it was pleasant enough and I could imagine it having a nice effect on the punters as she took their money. She asked me again who I was. I told her that Jack had sent me to help regarding last night's goings-on.

"Jack who?"

"Jack. As in your boss."

"First floor" and she buzzed me in.

Her flat door was ajar with a safety chain across it. She asked for ID. I gave her my driving licence. She peered at it then said,

"How do I know you are who you say you are? You could have got this with half a dozen Cornflake tokens."

"I don't eat breakfast." I held my mobile phone out to her with Jack's name and number in the window and told her to ring him. She slid the chain across and let me in.

She was tall, mid-twenties. She had a long slender face that ended in a cleft chin. She had large brown eyes with long black lashes and a smouldering sensuality behind them. Magenta-coloured hair cut short, boyish, though there was nothing boyish about her. There was a parting, then the hair was swept off her face to one side. I sniffed the perfume, sharp, classy, Miss D'Ore if I wasn't mistaken. And I'm usually not, because knowing your smellies can be handy in my line of work.

"Is there any news? Has anyone heard anything?"

"No," I lied.

"I was expecting the police. Why'd he send you?"

"He knows they're so busy these days. He didn't want to bother them."

"You don't do stand-up as well, do you?"

She wore tight-fitting grey running shorts that most guys would have done a four-minute mile to get inside of and a long-sleeved navy sweat top that almost covered her hands. There was a magnetism about her even for someone so young. It was the way she moved. As if she knew most blokes would like to jump her bones, so she had nothing to prove.

"Jack's asked me to help."

"Why hasn't anyone heard anything? Why isn't anyone doing anything? I'm really worried."

"They will."

She led me into her living room. Magnolia-painted walls with framed Warhol prints, Jackie Kennedy, Elvis, and lots of plants.

"Nice flat. Lived here long?"

"Nearly two years. But I spend time at Tony's as well."

"What happened?"

"You mean last night?" She padded barefoot over to a leather settee. She had such a lovely little arse it was a shame she had to sit on it. But she did, tucking long, long legs under her. "It's like I told Mister Kreeger. We left the

Freemont just after three. No one hearing anything is bad, isn't it?"

"Not necessarily. Go on."

"We parked up in the car park, were walking towards the flat. I asked him if he was hungry or was he going straight to bed. Then these guys came out of nowhere. It's getting on for four in the morning by then, right! Quiet everywhere, and it's like they weren't there. Then they were. One shoved me and I went sprawling, another put a hood over Tony's head and then they bundled him into a van and took off. I mean, the whole thing was over in seconds."

"How many guys?"

"Three. I think."

"Ever seen them before, at the casino maybe?"

"They wore masks."

"Did the van come in after you got out Tony's car? Or was it waiting?"

"I, I, I, I'm not sure. No. It must have been there already, or I'd have heard it."

"So they shoved Tony in the van, then what?"

"What d'you mean? Then what? I'm sprawled on the ground. What d'you think I did. Take out a pad and pencil and take notes! He will be okay, won't he?"

"Then what happened?"

"I asked you a question. Tony will be all right, won't he?"

"I hope so."

"Hope so?"

"What happened next?"

"I went up to the flat."

"How d'you get in?"

"I have keys, Colombo!" She rearranged herself on the settee. "I poured myself a drink, then rang Mister Kreeger at the casino."

"And?"

She told Jack what had happened and he and Terry had come over. I asked why she hadn't rung the police instead of Jack.

"Natural reaction, I suppose. Jack's his father, a shaker and a mover. Besides the impression I have of Mister Kreeger is that he doesn't do police, à la you!"

"You're pretty sharp, Zoe. Anyone ever tell you that?"

She pulled a face that was a kind of a physical sardonic version of 'you're too kind'. This one you just knew had had a lot of boyfriends and was used to them dancing to her tune.

"Please tell me he'll be okay."

"Me, Jack, Terry, we're doing all we can."

"Good. Thanks."

She said there was coffee on the go and asked if I wanted a cup. The kitchen was open-plan to the living room with a breakfast bar between, so she was able to talk while she poured. I noticed a small pink-coloured box marked Omeprazole at the end of it.

"You ill?"

She looked over and said, "No. They're Tony's. He has a stomach ulcer."

"Serious?"

"Only if he has a dodgy curry or too much to drink."

"Is he in trouble without them?"

"No. He can sort the pain with a pint of milk. But he prefers the capsules, especially if he has a bad episode. How d'you take your coffee? White or black?"

"White, two sugars please."

She came back in and handed me a mug.

"Tony rowed with anyone lately at the casino, or in his private life?"

"How would I know!"

"So after the attack you came back here, right?" She nodded.

"How?"

"Cab."

I took a sip of coffee. I didn't like the taste.

"Zoe Fontaine! That's quite a handle. Is that your real name?"

"Why, you going to do a police check on me like they do in the cop shows?"

"Would I find anything?"

"Only that I changed it. Because I'm an actress. Working nights means I can get to auditions."

"What was your name?"

"Doreen Entwhistle. I did it by deed poll. I mean, you can't see them at the Dolby in LA saying 'and best actress Oscar goes to Doreen Entwhistle', can you?" She drank some coffee and plonked the mug down on the bar. "There's no law against changing your name."

"Did I say there was?"

"I been on telly, you know. *Corrie*, and *The Bill* when it was running."

"How long ago?"

She studied her fingernails and said it had been a couple of years.

"Well, three maybe. I've done modelling in lads' mags. And TV ads," she added smiling. "I'm walking through Brent Cross Shopping Mall discussing my constipation with a girlfriend, like you do. Then there's a shot of me coming out of a pharmacy all happy and smiles and a voice-over says 'If your bowels are tight move them like clockwork with Shite Right' or whatever the hell the product was called," she added.

"I must have missed it. But then I don't have the problem."

"No. I don't suppose you do. You look pretty fit. What

are you, late thirties, forty?"

"Forty-one."

"You must work out. I go to a gym. I like watching the guys there, especially if they're good-looking, seeing the sweat run off their faces, down their bodies and biceps soaking into their singlets."

I imagined the sweat between us after a couple of hours in bed rolling between her breasts. Her back damp. The sheets moist. The fantasy was interrupted by her mobile.

"I'm busy. I can't talk. I'll ring you back." She clicked off and asked me if there was anything else.

"You definitely didn't see the guys that took Tony?"

"I told you. They wore masks."

"How long have you and Tony been dating?"

"About three months."

I imagined she'd seen Tony sweat quite a bit.

"And how long have you been at the Freemont?"

"A year or so."

"I guess that's it for the moment." I gave her my card and told her to ring if she thought of anything.

She flicked it with her well-manicured black painted thumbnail.

"Edward Sutton, Enquiry Agent and Certified Court Bailiff. Does that mean a private eye?"

"If you like," I said buttoning my jacket.

"Aren't you supposed to stop just before leaving, hold your fingers to your temple and say, 'Oh, yes! There was one other question, miss'?"

"You watch too much television, Zoe."

She gave me the face again. And I realised what it actually meant. Which was, fuck you!

I got to the door and stopped. There actually was one last question.

"Can I borrow Tony's flat keys for a couple of days?"

I sat in the Beema running the interview in my head. I wondered about their relationship. I caught my reflection in the driver's mirror. I suppose I wasn't in that bad a nick for forty-one. Six foot, blue eyes, no bags under them, square jaw, black cropped hair almost crew cut, not a strand of grey in it. Not bad looking. Quite handsome when you smile, an ex-girlfriend used to say. Well, even if I wasn't. At least I didn't scare the neighbours!

CHAPTER 3

Steve's snooker club in Kilburn High Road is where I hang out a lot. It's a good place for picking up gossip and getting the whereabouts of faces that need tracing. I walked down the avenue of tables to the refreshment bar from behind which Steve, an ex-copper friend of mine, who'd been my DCI at Mile Lane in the East End, runs his little gold mine. I sat on a bar stool and waited as he finished serving two guys in jeans with shaved heads. The smell of alcohol and sweat hung in the air. An explosion of laughter or swearing occasionally rising above the sound of voices and balls cracking against each other or cues rasping against tables, wood on wood.

"How you doing?"

"Not bad! You?" He pulled a pint and set it on the counter. "Want a game?"

"I'm working."

"Oh?"

"Got a call from Jack Kreeger."

"The Freemont Kreeger?" I nodded. "I thought he'd retired to Spain."

"That was his partner."

"Shows you how you lose touch."

"D'you ever have anything to do with him?"

"Nicked a bloke coming out of his casino once. That was, let's see. I've been out of it four years, so we're talking, oh a good while back." He wiped up some spilt beer and wrung the cloth out in a sink under the bar. "Four years. Jesus! Can you believe it!"

"Well, I've been out of it for five. So I suppose it must

be." I took a swig of the beer, enjoying getting rid of the taste of Zoe's coffee. "D'you miss it?" I asked.

"Not any more," he said, looking around the hall. "I did at first. Not easy making a new start." He stretched an arm out, embracing the hall. "Those bastards that broke my hands that night didn't know what a favour they were doing me. Ending up with all this." He looked at his fingers, which were long and thin with knuckles that sat a little too high on the surface, the index and the pinky even now not straight. "What about you?"

It was a question I asked myself often. What if I was still in the force? Maybe I'd have made DI by now. But I wouldn't have the kind of money I have. Or the flat. A smart three-bedroom conversion in Camden Town just on the edge of the West End. One end of the road leading to ever so sedate Regent's Park. The other end to Parkway, where for the price of a pint or a cappuccino, you can sit, take the weight off your feet and watch some serious talent strolling by. But I still miss the camaraderie. The Met's like a family. I have no parents alive. Only a younger brother. So no one older for support. I would like to have been part of a large family. Perhaps that's why I joined the force in the first place. That's maybe why Steve and I got on so well from day one. Because I saw him as an older sibling. Whatever it was, or is, I know I can trust him. He can trust me. He's balding now, poor sod. The dome of his head has hardly any hair on it. But it gets thicker to the sides and back. Black flecked with grey. Back then he was clean shaven. Nowadays he has a beard which matches his hair colouring. He has small dark eyes that don't miss a thing, set in a round face that smiles a lot.

"Anyway it was different for me," I said at last. "I never had an option."

"You was a good DC, Eddie. I still say they should have treated you better. You should have appealed."

"Against what? The guy ended up in hospital. It's all piss down the lav now, as far as I'm concerned!"

"There wasn't a copper in the nick that didn't want to give Farmer a right-hander or two."

"But it was me that did it."

"So why'd Jack ring you?"

I made sure there was no within earshot, leaned forwards and told him that someone had kidnapped his son, Tony.

"No shit!"

"He wants me to find him."

He poured himself a half, drank the head off and said,

"Don't get involved, Eddie."

"Too late. I've taken the king's shilling. Well, twenty-five grand actually."

"Fucking hell! Wake up, mate! He wouldn't have paid you that much if it was going to be a piece of piss."

And of course he was right. I saw that now. But twenty-five grand's twenty-five grand!

"It'll be all right. But I need to pick your brains."

He went off to serve a customer with a tea and a meat pie. Came back, took a sip of his beer and asked how.

"You still in contact with any snouts?"

"A couple from time to time. Why?"

"Anyone you can trust?"

"Maybe."

"If there's one, give him my number. I want to know what the gossip is about Jack, Tony, the Freemont." I finished my beer, offered to pay but he wouldn't take it.

"I should really, seeing as you're so flushed."

"See you later!"

"Eddie."

"Yeah?"

"Be careful mate."

CHAPTER 4

I went back to my office. Three first-floor rooms above a firm of accountants in Parkway, upon which I'd spent a fortune doing up. Expensive wood flooring, comfortable chairs from Heal's, good lighting, neutral magnolia decor. I like to live well, surround myself with nice things. If people come to an office that gives off good vibes, they're more likely to have confidence in you. At least, that's the theory. I made myself coffee, percolated, nice tasting unlike the rubbish at Zoe's. I saw her face in my mind's eye and understood why Tony would be keen on her regardless of Jack's objections to fraternising with the staff. Understood why I was keen on her. I got the keys to Tony's flat she'd given me and headed over to it in Kensington.

I stood in the car park of his block. The bays, numbered one to twelve marked out in white. Entrance in. Exit out. Come and go as you please. No gates. No electric operated arms. His flat was on the second floor. In the movies they open Yale locks with a credit card. In actual fact you need a piece of plastic, credit-card thick, about fifteen inches square. You slide it into the lock and shove the door with your shoulder at the same time. The easiest way, of course, of getting through a door is with keys, which why I'd borrowed his. It transpired I needn't have bothered with either key or plastic, because someone had jemmied it open and it just rested to. I pushed it with my foot and said a loud 'hello'. But there was no response. I said 'hello' again. Nothing, and I stepped gingerly inside.

There was a big hall with rooms off. The first I came to was the kitchen, ultra-modern with dark grey granite worktop surfaces. Granite-topped island. White wooden wall and floor units all open. All the crockery and cutlery had been turfed onto the floor, and boxes of cereal poured on top of them. The contents of the fridge were on the floor as well. As were the contents of the larder. The bathroom had had a medicine cabinet ripped off the wall and its contents including a box of Omeprazole strewn everywhere. And oddly enough an expensive-looking brown carpet pulled up at the corners.

I stepped cautiously into the bedroom, which had also had the treatment. It was a large bright room; there was a king-size bed with cream-coloured sheets and pillows that smelt of Zoe's perfume, strong, sharp, expensive, carrying the subliminal message of 'I can give you an erection to remember'. A mental image of them at it, her long legs wrapped around him, him thrusting, her laid back, taking it, flashed momentarily through my mind. Then I was back to the aggro. The mattress had been slashed. His suits and any clothing that had pockets had been pulled out of the wardrobes and cupboards and dumped, presumably after being searched. A bedside table's drawers had been pulled open, the contents – condoms, a football programme, a couple of hypodermics – scattered. The edges of the green carpet also lifted.

The living room had taken the worst of it with the soft furnishings and settees slashed. A room unit with TV and hi-fi yanked out of its housing, the contents of the shelves strewn everywhere. There were a couple of framed prints on the wall, a Lowry and a beach scene. I lifted them away with a penknife to look for a safe. But there wasn't one. Whatever had been sought had been well hidden, assuming it hadn't been found. It was small enough to hide in a cereal box or slide under the edge of a carpet. It wasn't money or drugs. So what, then? Jewellery? You wouldn't go to all that trouble. A ticket for something or photo? But for what. Or of what?

I went back into the other rooms, but couldn't see where else you could hide something small that hadn't been searched. The best place to secrete something from someone is right under their nose. That's what made me look at the walls. I banged a couple. But they were solid. I stood there in the middle of it all, looking at the chaos, glad it wasn't my place. I started to leave. Stood in the hall for one last glance and noticed there were three lots of double power points. Three didn't strike me as odd, just a bit over the top for a hall perhaps. Then I noticed the middle one sitting slightly crooked compared with the other two. I tapped the facia with my penknife. Hollow. There was a hairline gap between it and the wall, only visible if you really put your nose to it. I stuck the blade in the gap and pulled and a drawer slid out from the wall. I'd heard of these dummy power point hiding boxes. But never actually seen one. It was cute and clever and I thought I might get one for myself.

There was something wrapped in a blue check tea towel. I opened it to find a Colt .38 snub-nosed revolver, nicknamed the Detective Special. It was black with a walnut hand-grip. I knew a lot about the snub-nose. Because I owned one myself that I kept wrapped in foil hidden in a cheese box in my fridge. The six chambers were empty. But there was a box of shells beside it. I left it as found and slid the power point facia back into place, wondering why a rich, middle-class 28-year-old would have a gun hidden in his flat.

CHAPTER 5

Jack had mentioned that Davina, Ronnie's daughter, and Tony were close. So I decided to check her out. I rang her three times, only getting voicemail. So I decided to call on her. Her address was a very expensive and exclusive mews flat in Bayswater. As I parked, it was clear something was wrong. But I had no reason to think it was to do with her. There were police vans kerb to kerb, either end. And a silver-grey BMW police response nearby. Blue-and-white police scene-of-crime tape secured lamppost to lamppost and in front of that a ROAD CLOSED notice board with a couple of PCs in hi-vis vests milling around as another couple with clipboards knocked on doors.

I walked casually along, planning to slip through a gap between lamppost and wall. I knew I'd be challenged but I had a story prepared.

She was twenty-something, a little tubby with a wisp of blond hair sticking out from under her cap.

"Sorry, sir. You can't come through unless you live here."

"I do. That's to say, I'm staying with a friend, Davina Miller, number five."

"Sutton!" boomed a voice. I turned in its direction. "What you doing here?" It belonged to Tom Stafford, a DCI from Kensington nick whom I'd known for several years. "Well, well, well! Where there's trouble you'll find Eddie Sutton. They go together like peaches and cream, Sherlock and Holmes."

"That should be Holmes and Watson!"

"What are you, a fucking literary expert all of a sudden?"

"How are you, Detective Inspector?"

"All the worse for seeing you!" I stretched out my hand. He took it and smiled.

He wasn't as tall as me. But what he lacked in height he made up for in presence. A bull of a man with a barrel chest. We ran across each from time to time when we were involved in the same bit of business but in different ways. And helped each other if we could. Me supplying him with bits of gossip I'd picked up about aggro committed on his manor. The whereabouts of faces. Who was drinking with whom lately. Not regularly; but often enough to get a favour or two when needed. I liked him and his sarcastic sardonic attitude to the world. I wasn't sure if he liked me. Maybe the best anyone could expect was to be suffered by him.

"Let me take a wild guess, Eddie. You're visiting number five."

"How d'you …?"

He told the WPC to let me through the tape. Then beckoned me to follow past a PC standing guard outside the front door.

"Holmes and fucking Watson," he mumbled under his breath.

Her flat consumed the whole of the ground floor of the house. He led me through a large square hall of jade and gold-coloured tiled flooring lit up by a three-tier crystal chandelier that would have put the sun to shame. Her bedroom was even larger than the hall. It had cream-coloured velvet banquet seating skirting the walls. Long arch-shaped windows framed in matching velvet ceiling-to-floor curtains. Gold-coloured wall lights holding long imitation candles with clear bulbs atop of them and to one side a huge Adam fireplace, beside a seven-foot-square bed.

She lay on the floor propped against a wardrobe like a Guy Fawkes. Legs outstretched, arms either side resting on the beige carpet. Her head flopped to one side, eyes closed. There were cuts to her cheeks and the bruising around her jaw was dark mauve with tiny irregular vermilion shapes in it. Her long auburn hair was dishevelled. She had a round face, long slender nose and full wide lips. Fluid had dripped from them and dried on her chin. Because bodily fluid drains out of a cadaver whichever way it can. Some of it had dripped onto her green silk shirt, leaving light-grey streaks down it. And all around her there was movement and industry. SOCOs in white boiler suits with tweezers and small brushes and polythene bags. But nobody touching her, flashbulbs exploding as others photographed everything. Two guys in plain clothes, CID, talking to a WPC. And in the centre of the room a uniformed inspector watching that everything was being done correctly.

"The doc reckons she's been here about a day. Reckons she was punched a couple of times. One of the punches sent her backwards and fractured her skull on the corner of the wardrobe."

"Who found her?"

"She has a woman comes in once a week, cleaning, laundry, bit of shopping. She was loading the dishwasher, came in here to see if there was any crockery and nearly had a fit.. I've got a WPC giving her TLC in the kitchen. Poor cow! What a way to start the day!"

"Forced entry?"

"No."

"She couldn't have been more than twenty-five, twenty-six," I said for no particular reason

"Twenty-seven."

Tony kidnapped. His friend dead. Murdered, as throwing yourself against a wardrobe isn't a usual way of committing suicide. It didn't necessarily follow her murder was connected to Jack's bit of business. I told myself. It could realistically be connected with any number of things to do with her life. But I'm not a fan of coincidences. There was no point in me staying. I knew the form. I'd only be in the way so I said,

"Thanks for letting me in. I'll let your people get on with it." I was waiting for the question. Because that's why he'd allowed me access. I got as far as the door when it came.

"By the way, Eddie! Why'd you want to see her?"

"To offer my condolences for her father." I couldn't tell if he believed me.

 He gave me his usual hangdog expression

"You knew her then?"

"I knew Ronnie."

"Why didn't you ring?"

"I did. But just kept getting voicemail."

He nodded in the stern and thoughtful way coppers do. And I knew he absolutely didn't believe a word of it.

CHAPTER 6

I phoned Ricky Houston and told him that I wanted to see him at noon. It wasn't convenient. I said that was too bad. Because Jack, as his employer, had asked me to call. As it turned out I got there a half hour earlier than I'd expected.

He lived on the ground floor of a purpose-built block on the Cromwell Road. I buzzed, gave him my name. He said whatever I was selling to clear off.

"The name's Sutton. I phoned."

There was a guy in his late twenties in jeans and a leather bomber jacket walking away from Ricky's door. I stepped aside but not quickly enough, because we banged shoulders. He said sorry without turning around, grabbed the front door and slammed it behind him.

Ricky Houston was slim, about six foot. He stood in the doorway, one arm on the doorpost.

"Is this going to take long? I have company."

"Tell them your uncle from Guatemala's turned up. Get rid of them."

He pushed the door open and I followed him through a small hall and down some steps into the living room. His company was a man called Lenny Jordan, a small-time professional thief and safecracker whom I had nicked so many times that if there was a Lonsdale Belt for arrests I would have owned him. He was sitting on a settee in creased trousers and a high-collared donkey jacket, one arm along the upright, while he picked his teeth with his free hand. He looked at what he'd extracted, then sucked it off his finger.

"This is …"

"I know. I've had the pleasure and believe me it's no pleasure. I didn't know you were out, Jordan."

"Early release. I've decided to go straight."

"Yeah, right! That would be like trying to restore virginity!"

"Up yours, Sutton!"

I pulled him off the settee with a fistful of his lapel. He put his hands up, protecting the hooked nose, the thin lips. Ricky stepped between us and pushed me away.

"Enough! Lenny, I think you'd best go. I'll ring you."

Jordan straightened his jacket, looked me up and down and headed for the door.

Ricky asked how I knew Jordan and sniffed.

"I've nicked him a few times for burglary over the years."

"Oh, police, right! I didn't realise."

"Used to be. You keep bad company, Mister Houston."

"My company, my business! This call's about Tony, right?" and he sniffed again, then ran a hand over his stubbled chin. He flopped onto the settee and put his feet up on a long teak coffee table.

"I understand Tony's a good friend of yours. Known him long?"

"About eighteen months. Since I started working at the Freemont. I know he's been snatched." He sniffed again through nostrils that were puffed and red at the edges. I thought he had a cold, then he sniffed again and I realised he was a user. Probably coke. Too much up the nose destroys the septum and that makes you sniff a lot, just the way Ricky did. Jack said he was thirty. But the bags under his small eyes and alabaster complexion made him look older.

"How d'you know?" I asked.

"Zoe!"

"So she probably told you I'd be calling."

"She said you'd be sniffing around."

"There's sniffing and there's sniffing, isn't there, Ricky?"

"Anything else, Mister Sutton?" he said, emphasising the mister.

"Where d'you know Jordan from?"

"He's a friend of a friend."

I asked him if Tony had any enemies. Anyone who might want to harm him to the point he felt he needed protection. He shook his head.

"Jack been involved in any aggro at the club?"

"Not to my knowledge. Why don't you ask his henchwoman."

"Maxine Andrews?"

"Yeah! Fucking Maxine!"

"When d'you last see him?"

"The evening it happened."

"What time did you leave the Freemont?"

"Four-ish."

"And Tony's had no beef with anyone? A punter losing money at his tables? Or a problem with an ex-boyfriend of Zoe's perhaps?" He shook his head and said 'none'.

"Okay, Ricky. I'll be in touch if I need to speak to you again."

"I can't wait!"

CHAPTER 7

I came out of Houston's trying to make my mind up about him. He might be on coke. But then so was half the country. It didn't prove anything. I thought about whether if you were going to snatch Tony you'd need someone to mark your card. Let you know what evening he was there and what time he was leaving. Someone like Ricky would be useful. Or Zoe!

I turned the corner. The sun was out. But a breeze cancelled the warmth. I'd gone about thirty yards when I noticed the guy I'd bumped shoulders with in the corridor outside Ricky's flat. He had the hood up of a navy Porsche 911.

"Trouble?"

He turned around. Brown eyes, in a round face, with rosy cheeks stared back.

"Sorry?"

"We met in the corridor, sort of, over there," I said, pointing to Ricky's block.

"Oh, yeah."

"Where d'you know Ricky from?"

"I don't. Not really. I was just enquiring about a friend of mine, if it's any of your business."

"Wouldn't be Tony Kreeger, would it?"

He turned his attention from the car to me.

"And if it was? What's that got to do with you?"

"Tony's got himself in a bit of bother. Jack's asked me to help."

"What d'you say your name was?"

"Eddie Sutton. And you are?"

"Mike Lane. A friend of Tony's. You work for Jack, do you?"

"Sort of."

"What kind of trouble?"

"Nothing that won't get sorted."

"You sure you work for Jack?"

I scrolled Jack's number on my mobile and told him to ring it. He went through the usual hellos and how was he. Then said he was with a guy called Eddie Sutton who was asking about Tony.

"Yeah!" he said, giving me the once-over again. "About six foot, slim, black cropped hair, reckons himself if you ask me. If you're sure. Speak soon."

"Okay?" I said.

"I suppose so," and handed me back my phone. "We've been friends since we were kids. I mean, we were like brothers. Then he started running around with a bit of an iffy crowd doing drugs. I mean heavy stuff not just joints. We lost touch. We were supposed to do lunch the other day. He didn't turn up. And nothing since. I've tried calling him but there's not even a dialling tone. I know Ricky's a pal of his, and I knew where he lived because Tony took me to a poker evening at Houston's a couple of times. So I thought I'd call and see if he knew anything."

"And did he?"

He shook his head.

"And couldn't get rid of me quick enough."

"This lunch was for what, catching up?"

He moved a step closer and asked again what kind of trouble Tony was in.

"Can't really say. But anything you can tell me that will help would be really welcome."

"What's he done; knocked up one of the croupiers?"

"No, nothing like that."

He looked me up and down as if he were deciding about something then said,

"Jack's all right. He and my dad go way back. But if I tell you something it's on the basis it's between you and me. Right?"

"Depends. Is it criminal?"

"No."

"Go on."

"Tony borrowed twenty grand off me. Don't tell Jack. Because if he knew he'd go ballistic."

"I can keep a secret. Why'd he want it?"

"Just said he was in a jam. He looked different."

"Different?"

"Anxious, nervous. Like he could do with a week's sleep and a good holiday." He shrugged and added, "Maybe it's just too much coke and too much pussy. I tell you, man, that casino is like a pussy Aladdin's cave."

He stuck his head under the bonnet and pulled at a couple of wires and something sparked. Then he sat in the car, turned the ignition and the engine purred.

"Nice one!"

"Haven't found an engine to beat me yet."

"You in the business?"

"Yeah. My old man's Harry Lane." He saw it wasn't registering and said, "Second-hand cars. We've got half a dozen showrooms around London. You must have heard our ad 'When it comes to used cars. Get into the right lane for a great deal'. There's sound effects with it. You know, like F1s revving." It rang a bell.

"So Tony, with all his money, was borrowing."

"'Fraid so. And not just off me. He tapped another friend of ours for five."

"And you've no idea why?"

"Like I said. I've known him long enough to know it

must have been important if he didn't want to say. It was all right with me. I know he's good for it. I'll get it back. Is he in trouble with the cops?"

I shook my head.

"You've been a great help. Thanks."

"What I told you is between you and me. Got it?"

"Absolutely." I gave him my number. He clicked it into his mobile. I told him to ring me if he thought of anything else.

"What you driving?" he asked.

"Beema. Series three."

"What's the condition like?"

"It's almost new, starts first time every time. Just like me."

He smiled and said,

"If you fancy a change, I'll give you a good deal" and he handed me his card.

CHAPTER 8

Two armour-plated glass doors slid aside. You went up six black thickly carpeted stairs and you were at the reception area of the Freemont Casino, where a couple of evening-suited bouncers with starched shirts and starched smiles said 'good evening' and directed you to a brunette in a black evening dress sitting behind a long desk. Everyone was in evening wear. I was glad now I'd made the effort, because I like dressing up and I don't often get the opportunity. I've got a good wardrobe. I don't buy cheap stuff. The leather jacket I'd worn to Jack's house had cost three hundred quid. But a dress suit, that makes you feel real posh.

I gave the girl my name and she smiled a cute little smile with dimples and said she'd been told I would be coming. I filled out a form, had a digital photo taken and was told membership would be ready in a jiffy. Meantime I was to be taken up to Mister Kreeger's office. She caught the eye of a bouncer and I was escorted. We walked through a huge ground-floor gaming room, past a bow shaped bar of about twenty feet with a mirrored wall behind it and glass shelves upon which sat maybe a couple of hundred different bottles of everything I'd ever drunk, heard of or seen advertised.

The gaming tables, arranged in no particular order, were kidney-shaped, leather-edged. The croupiers behind them, mainly girls in black evening dresses, were watched by male dress-suited pit bosses with sphinx-like expressions. Watching, watching, always watching. I spotted Zoe behind one of the tables across the way busy dealing cards. The room was bathed in bright white light from large beautiful crystal chandeliers, with dozens and dozens of crystal droplets shaped like petals that sparkled and flashed light into every corner. The walls were papered in pale pink flock wallpaper. Not your Indian restaurant stuff. More your two-hundred-pound-a-roll gear. It was all breathtakingly exquisite. It didn't matter the game black-jack, roulette, craps — all the seats around the tables were occupied. One woman at poker kissed a chip, touched it to a crucifix hanging around her neck then placed it. And I couldn't help but think it was going to take more than Jesus to beat this house. More like a card sharp. In which case, Jesus would be dealing with a den of sleeves.

The areas between the tables ebbed and flowed with people. The men in either single- or double-breasted dinner suits. The women cool, gowned, groomed, bejewelled, moneyed, delicious. It was a moving pattern of people. A kaleidoscope of wealth. We passed the first floor. There was an arch leading through to a large restaurant. Candlelit tables, white linen tablecloths, silver cutlery, soft music; the waiters in dress suits. Not a table to be had.

There were two rooms at the beginning of the second. One with a locked gate across it. Which is where I supposed the money was. The other marked NO ENTRY with voices behind it, which I guessed was security monitoring the CCTV. There were swing doors at the end of the corridor and offices beyond. The bouncer knocked on one. Jack said 'yes' from the other side and I was ushered in.

He sat behind a large desk. Not as big as the one in his library. But big enough. It had a computer screen on it and four telephones. To his left was a wall of split CCTV screens providing pictures of everything and everywhere and underneath them a bank of filing cabinets.

"Looks like NATO Headquarters."

"The TVs, you mean. I like to see what's going on." He put a finger to his lips and snatched open the office door. But there was no one outside. "I heard about Davina," he said, resuming his seat. "So sad. I remember when she was born. She was the apple of Ronnie's eye. So, so sad!"

"Yeah, nasty," I replied, taking a chair opposite. "I saw the body. Not nice!"

"How come?"

I told him.

"They're saying it was murder."

"Maybe."

He sighed a deep sigh, and slowly shook his head.

"I only saw her a week ago. You know."

"Oh?"

"She came to see me. Sat right where you are."

"What about?"

"Ostensibly Ronnie's funeral."

"Ostensibly?"

"Drink? You eaten? D'you want a meal in the restaurant? On the house."

"Drink's fine. Scotch, with a little water, please."

He slid open a false bookcase of brown leather books. All the same size, all perfectly regimented in a line set in a wall and revealing a stack of bottles and glasses; he poured me one.

"Tony and I are sitting here one afternoon discussing something or other," Jack said, "and they buzz me from reception to say she's downstairs and wants a word. In she flounces, looking very well and beautifully turned out like she always did. Designer label suit, black leather coat, black patent high heels. But then she always was chic. The word is, about Ronnie's funeral. Am I going? I told her I hadn't made up my mind. She says of course she is." He poured himself a Scotch and sat there rocking the glass as if he were trying to remember everything that had happened. " 'The thing is, Uncle Jack, she continues.' She always called me Uncle Jack. 'Anyway. Daddy's left a will. I'll be talking to solicitors as I've heard on the grapevine I'm a beneficiary. I was wondering if you think he may have left you anything?' I ask why she wants to know. 'Because if there is anything for you, I could bring it back with me. It would save you a hassle and getting involved with paperwork.' "

He walked over to the TV screens and stared at them, then moved along the line, smiling.
"Isn't it nice when you see lots of people losing lots of their money to you!"
"Great!"
"This is one of the last independent casinos left in the West End. I'm beholden to no one. No Board of Directors. No shareholders. There's just me. Which is where all the money comes to." He nodded slowly, as though congratulating himself. "Where was I. Oh, yes! I was actually on the point of saying 'yes' to her. But she seemed too anxious for me to agree, pointing out all the benefits and the conveniences. Then she pulls a letter from her handbag for me to sign for the solicitors in Spain, giving her authority to bring my stuff back. That's when I said 'no'."
"What did she say?"
"She backed off. Said she was just trying to be helpful."
I took a sip of the Scotch and sat back in the chair.
"She ask about travelling together if you were going?"
He shook his head.
"So not that interested in you then."
I finished my drink and asked him when he was

expecting Ronnie's stuff. He said in a couple of days.

"You look troubled, Eddie. What's on your mind?"

"There's something not right about all this."

"In which way?"

"I don't know."

"You don't think my Tony's …?"

"No. He's safe. So long as they don't have the book."

"You sure. I can't tell you how much the worry and the anxiety is beginning to get to me."

"He's safe at the moment."

"Let's hope so. Because both Carlin and Doorrell are vicious bastards. Particularly Doorrell."

"So you said."

"He's been after this casino for ages. Four weeks ago he made a new move on me. He managed to buy the freehold of the building here. I'd been after it myself for years. But the owner wouldn't sell it to me."

"So how did he get it?" I asked.

Jack shrugged.

"Probably got a couple of his tarts to set him up in a compromising position. And they would if they were ordered to. Because Doorrell has a reputation for being brutal with his girls. Then he probably blackmailed the owner into selling. Usual thing. Threaten to send photos or videos to his wife and family. Or put it out on YouTube."

"I don't see your problem. You have a lease, don't you?"

"No, you don't see it," he said finishing his drink. "If he can prove serious drug dealing here, because he's obviously not going to mention prostitution, he can go to court and ask for the confiscation of the lease. He then gets the Freemont and I get stuffed. And what better evidence would you need than something in the actual handwriting of the ex-owner?"

I didn't say anything. But this rich pimp as Jack described him struck me as being quite a clever little bastard. Clever and vicious! Not good!

There was a knock on the door. Jack said 'yes'. She was blonde, but she'd had help. There was one button too many undone of her cream silk shirt revealing nice cleavage, bringing a whole new meaning to the phrase Silicone Valley!

"Your membership card and literature about the Freemont, Mister Sutton. We hope you enjoy the Freemont experience."

"I'm sure I will." I put the card in my wallet and watched her wiggle her way out.

"Just love your staff, Jack!"

"I'm so pleased. Talking of which, when you've picked your tongue up off the floor, I'll take you next door and introduce you to my General Manager."

CHAPTER 9

Maxine Andrews had big blue eyes, and a nice smile right across an egg-shaped face of flawless skin. She wore black horn-rimmed glasses on the bridge of a tiny nose and looked over them to see what Jack had brought in. She came around her desk and offered her hand. A cool, slim, pink nail-varnished job.

"Mister Sutton."

I looked for a wedding ring. I always look for a wedding ring. But there wasn't one. So I emphasised the ms.

"Ms Andrews. Nice to meet you." And it was. Very nice. Even with glasses.

"I'll leave the two of you," Jack said.

"Jack told me you wanted a word," she began, as the door closed, in a voice low and husky. "I'd want to help, whichever way I can. So?" She slid a chair over for me from beside a wall with a mirror hanging on it.

"You have more to do with Tony on a day-to-day basis than most. So I thought I might get some background from you."

"In which way?"

"Any enemies here?"

She went back to her desk. But not before removing the specs. She had ash-blond hair, the sides separated by a centre parting then combed back and secured with a slide. She flicked at a couple of wayward strands by her ear in the reflection of the mirror.

"I have a problem with Tony."

"Oh?"

"I'm his boss. I'm supposed to be training him up for management. But he's Jack's son and that trumps me."

"What does that mean exactly?"

She drummed her fingers on the desk. Pink-coloured nails clicked against the wood. Click, click, click!

"How much of what I say gets back to Jack?"

"Nothing."

"Honest?"

"You have my word."

She peered at me. I got the impression she made up her mind about people from her gut instinct rather than whatever she saw with the specs.

"You're sure about that, Mister Sutton, are you?"

"I used to be an estate agent. Would I lie to you!"

A smile crossed her lips.

"Well, I suppose one can't ask for any greater assurance than that" she said sarcastically. "If I had my way I'd fire him!"

"Because?"

"He's lazy and a bully. If he was any good at his job I might get past it. But he's not. But he's Jack's son."

"How do they get on?"

"I think they have their problems. He seems jealous of what Jack's achieved. Because he just doesn't have it."

"It?"

"Savvy, street smart." She shrugged in an embarrassed sort of way, then added, "Then there's me. I must resemble an impediment to his future."

"So. Just an everyday story of Knightsbridge folk!" I replied.

Her phone buzzed. A voice said, "Boss. The Fulltons are in; one wants two grand credit."

"The younger or the elder?"

"Elder."

"Tell them I said okay." She replaced the receiver and turned those blue eyes back onto me.

"How long have you been here?" I asked.

"Seven months." She told me how Jack had brought her in after he got back into things following Kitty, his wife's, death and discovered what was going on. That the place had been a mess. And that she'd cleaned it up with his help and backing. "I fired two people the second day I was here. And another three at the end of my first week."

"Really!"

"It sent out two messages. The first. That I know this business inside out. So don't mess with me."

"And the second?"

"That I don't take shit from any one!" and in that voice of hers it sounded even more threatening than it otherwise would have. She'd fired five people in seven days. And she might just as well have been talking about the weather.

"Why'd you fire them?"

"The first two were quite unnecessarily rude to customers. The other three were thieving."

I wondered if any of the five might have had a grudge. But she was ahead of me.

"I don't think they'd have been involved in anything like this."

"You sound like a real toughie, Ms Andrews, if you don't mind me saying."

"I was one of the top managers from the biggest national chain of casinos. I've straightened this place out so that it's straight, clean and runs like clockwork. Doing that is bound to upset some people. Don't get me wrong. I care about the people I care about I suppose I just don't care about people I don't care about, if that makes sense!"

It made sense all right. When she said 'don't mess with

me', even in that velvety, honey-dripping voice, that's exactly what she meant.

"No offence, I still don't think I'd like to bump into you in a dark alley!"

She sat looking at me. Just staring for a few seconds without blinking. I was expecting something sarcastic even vitriolic when she said,

"You should reserve judgment, Mister Sutton. There's all sorts of things happen in dark alleys!"

I had a ten-second fantasy about us in a dark alley. Her against a wall. Skirt around her waist, panties down and I wished I had time to spin ten seconds into ten minutes.

"So no ex-employees then. What about enemies?"

"More likely. I should think he had quite a few." She went over to a filing cabinet and withdrew some papers. She was slim, a couple of inches shorter than me and I guessed a couple of years younger. She came back to the desk and said she had to make a quick phone call, pressed a couple of buttons and asked someone for some figures to compare with last week's totals.

"As quick as you like, please! When new management takes over," she said, returning her attention to me, "staff split two ways. They're either hostile or go out of their way to ingratiate themselves with you. From the latter you get stuff it would have taken you weeks and weeks to discover for yourself."

"Which was?"

"Ronnie was using the place for drug dealing. I don't mean the odd deal. I mean serious, high-profit, ongoing, big money business."

"And you think Tony knew?"

"He said he didn't. But how could he not. Maybe someone doesn't like the business ending."

And if that someone was Danny Carlin, I told myself, which it was, he certainly would not have liked it ending.

Because he was a bit of a magician was Danny, in that people who upset him or got in his way he made disappear. And if he didn't wave the 'magic wand' himself, he left it to Collette Hammond, a female interrogator who worked for him. Either way it ended up with 'now you see them, and now you don't'.

"I've spoken with a couple of Tony's friends. Ricky Houston and a Zoe Fontaine," I said.

"Lucky you!"

"You're not a fan?"

"She's a great croupier. Quick hands, mind like a calculator, great with the customers. But not my cup of tea." Ricky didn't get off so lightly either on the Andrews popularity scale. "If he left tomorrow, it wouldn't be any great loss."

I was going to tell her she didn't mince her words. But she didn't need telling.

"And he's a sneak," she added. "He kept coming in late. So I bawled him out. Instead of standing up to me, he went to Tony who took it to Jack."

"What did Jack say?"

"That if he stopped being late, there wouldn't be a problem. And don't go behind my back again."

She pushed her chair away from her desk and said what must I think of her manners and offered me a drink.

"Tea, coffee. Something stronger?"

"That's kind of you. But I had one in Jack's office. Besides, I think we're done."

"If you're sure."

"Thanks anyway. And thanks for the heads up."

"My pleasure. If you need me again, you know where I am."

We shook hands. I headed for the door. She was back on the phone.

"Where are those figures, Michael? Don't give me busy, please. This is Maxine you're talking to."

On the phone she might have been. But as I opened the door, I noticed in the reflection of the mirror she was still looking at me.

I went back to Jack to tell him I was off.

"Everything okay with Maxine?"

"Fine."

"She's a real sweety, don't you think?"

I said yes. But a whole load of other adjectives also went through my mind.

I went home. I was hungry. I mulled things over, with a sandwich and a cup of coffee. Jack fancied either Danny or Doorrell. Both good prime suspects. Well, whoever it was we'd know soon, because they'd have to show their hands once we had the book. I wondered again why Tony would have a gun, and need to borrow money. Then she popped into my head. Tall, attractive Maxine. I smiled, thinking about the repartee regarding dark alleys. Was there more to it? Or was she just being clever? No wedding ring. What did that imply? And found myself hoping she wasn't gay. Divorced? Widowed? Widows usually continued to wear their rings. Maybe just a very cool, good-looking spinster. Just because you're an unmarried female, doesn't mean to say you're into car maintenance and DIY. Then I remembered her removing her specs and flicking quickly at her hair in the mirror . She cared about how men saw her. My money was on divorced.

CHAPTER 10

There was hardly anyone at Steve's. A couple of lads arguing in hushed tones over a snooker point. The sound of balls cracking from another table bounced in the emptiness.

"Wanna a game?"

"Why not! And a half." He poured me one and turned the lights on over table six.

"You're going to get a call from a bloke named Arnie. Used to be a snout of mine. He still has his ear to the ground. If there's any gossip, he'll know."

"How far can I trust him?"

"He's a snout! Sandwich?"

"Ham."

"I got cheese, cheese and pickle, cheese and tomato."

"Anything with cheese in it will do."

"Good choice!" While he was getting it, I phoned Zoe to find out exactly what she'd told Ricky. And to tell her to keep her mouth shut in future. But I just got voicemail.

I took my drink and cheese and pickle sandwich and plonked them on a windowsill by table six. My best ever was one, two, five. A hundred and forty-seven has always been beyond me. The cue ball split the reds nicely. I sank one with a second shot. I lined up the black; my mobile trilled. It was Tom Stafford.

"Thought I'd say hello, Eddie."

"Hello."

"Wondered if you'd heard anything about the Miller

girl?" he asked.

"Nothing. You?"

"The quack was right. She died from a fractured skull. The post-mortem found high levels of coke in her blood. And I don't mean the cola variety. Turns out she had form. A caution in 2010 for personal use. Arrested together with a bloke called Richard Houston."

"What's the story on this Richard Houston guy?"

"We're checking on him."

While I'm listening to Stafford, I'm wondering if gear's the reason for her being croaked. No false entry at her flat. So she knew who she was letting in. Then again, I'm not a great believer in coincidences. So when Ronnie Miller's daughter turns up dead just after Ronnie's personal stuff comes to light, well, call me paranoid but that doesn't mean to say that there's not something nasty and evil afoot!

"You still there?" Stafford asked.

"Yes."

"What d'you think?"

"What's her background?"

"Property developer. Ran a firm called Residential Dreams. Good stuff. Notting Hill, Kensington. Has offices in Shepherd's Bush Road." I took down the address and then some beer. "Not short of a bob or two. Seems like the developments are self-financed." He paused for a moment as if he couldn't make up his mind about saying something.

"Chief Inspector?"

"I did a Companies House search on the firm. She has a fellow 50 per cent director."

"Ronnie Miller?"

"Danny Carlin."

I opened my mouth. But nothing came out. I just stood there with a gob full of cheese and pickle and the phone at my ear.

"Still there?"

"Still here." But my voice didn't sound right.

"So we have a corpse that had a habit. That owned a company with some very bad company. Tell me again why you went to see her, Eddie?"

I took a long gulp of my drink and said,

"To offer my condolences about Ronnie."

"Oh, yeah! That's right, you said. And you rang but kept getting voicemail. I think you and I should meet for a chat, Eddie."

"Why?"

"So you can tell me what the fuck's going on."

"There's nothing."

"Bollocks! That's Metropolitan Police jargon for don't take the piss. Or insult my intelligence."

"Such a short word for such a big definition!"

"Tomorrow 9.30 a.m. Kensington nick." It didn't sound like a request.

I took another swig of my beer and a lump out of the sandwich. I saw Davina in my mind's eye, on the floor propped up against the wardrobe. She looked good even as a corpse. So she must have been a looker when she was breathing. Her death was the by-product of something, because you didn't set out to murder someone by punching them. But a by-product of what? I wondered about Ricky and her. Perhaps he'd gone round there for drugs and things had gone wrong. Then Tom Stafford popped into my head. He was going to be a problem. I'd known him for two or three years. We'd met when we crossed paths on a case of mine and became strong acquaintances. I slipped him information from time to time to oil the wheels of co-operation for those occasions an ex-Met officer needs a favour from a serving one. He was originally mistrustful of me thinking I'd been sacked for being on the take. But warmed when he discovered it was for putting a drug dealer in hospital. Something I suspected he'd like to do to all drug dealers himself. He was copper through and through. Who knew when to be hard, and when to cut some slack. Medium height, barrel-chested, not the sort of person you'd start a row with. Not if you had any sense that is.

I took a shot at the black. It rolled across the table, and rested at the jaw of a pocket. I kicked the table leg and it went in. Well ... why not! My game. My money! I tried Zoe again. No answer. I went back to the balls. But found I'd lost interest. So I decided to go to Shepherd's Bush. I sat in the Beema and lit up, mulling things over. One dead. One missing, that might turn up dead. Twenty-five grand suddenly didn't seem so much after all for this little caper.

CHAPTER 11

Robin Montague was about forty. He had bloodshot eyes from either rubbing them or crying.

"I still can't get over it! I can't tell you how distraught I was. How distraught we all still are," he said, sweeping a hand around the office that embraced two secretaries and a bookkeeper. So I guessed it was from crying. "She was such a lovely person. And to have died like, like, the way she … Just awful. Just so, so awful."

Davina's place was in fact a converted shop partitioned into four offices. Two large ones, hers, and Robin's where a computer and a large drawing board table, chair and desk resided. And two smaller ones for the staff.

"I joined the firm about three years ago, handling the professional side. The architecture, design, and dealing with planning. She was doing so well. She wanted someone in-house." He carried two cups of percolated coffee over and set them down on his desk. He sat on a chair and crossed one leg in very, very tight-fitting brown corduroy trousers over the other. "Help yourself to sugar."

"So a pretty successful operation then?"

"Very. And from nothing. She was a frustrated estate agent negotiator just up the road in Hammersmith. Her father …" he paused to ask me if I knew who Ronnie was, "wanted her to go into the casino business. But she had other ideas." He picked up his cup with two fingers and a thumb with the pinky stretched at right angles and took the smallest of sips. "She found a run-down property in Acton," he said, brushing a sandy-coloured fringe off his forehead. "Acton, I ask you, of all places," he added with a little laugh, as though the idea of anyone living in Acton was incomprehensible. "Three self-contained flats. Made a killing; never looked back."

"And now it's Kensington."

"High profile. High profit." He told me about her amazing taste, and aptitude for creating space. Mezzanine floors, roof terraces. "She told me how she saw it and wanted it. And I put pen to paper so to speak to make it materialise."

"What'll happen now?"

"I have a meeting with the other director tomorrow."

"Danny Carlin."

"You know him?"

"Oh, yeah!"

"He sounded pretty cut up on the phone."

"Really?"

"They were close, you know. Not an item. But I think they had their moments," he added with a wink.

I took a swig of the coffee, dying for a fag.

"Their moments?"

"You could tell. The following morning after a date with him, she was full of beans and he used to send her flowers. Roses. Beautiful roses. They're my favourite flowers are roses."

He told me how they'd met from a chance moment. Builders had let her down and someone had recommended Carlin and they'd just hit it off.

"He did a great job for her. Then another, and another."

"Just one erection after another, so to speak!"

"Sorry! Then a joint venture. Her property. His building input. Then as far as I can tell, Mister Carlin put a load of money into the business for a 50–50 share and that took us right into the big time. Buy what you like. No need for funding. No need to go arse-kissing the banks."

"Did Danny say what might happen?"

He shook his head. I wondered if half a successful business was worth killing for.

"I understand Davina wasn't long back from Spain?" I said.

"Yes. Mister Miller's funeral. Sixty-three, makes you think," he said, touching a green-and-blue polka-dot bow tie that fitted perfectly into the collar of his pale green shirt.

"Did Danny go with her?"

"She went alone. Though a friend of hers, Tony something, kept wanting to go with her to pay his last respects. He kept pressing and pressing her." Robin went over to the percolator and poured himself another and asked if I wanted. But I declined. "It ended in quite a scene. Just over there by the computer."

"What happened?"

"She said, and I quote, 'I'm going on my own. Now fucking well let it go!' She doesn't mince her words. Does our Davina ... Didn't."

"And did he?"

"Did he what?"

"Let it go?"

He shrugged and said,

"I suppose so. Because he turned up here the day she came back with the biggest bunch of flowers by way of an apology. And they both seemed, you know, lovey-dovey. Except ..."

"Except?"

"Come to think of it," he said, taking another moment or two to think. He blew on the coffee, then taking a sip added, "He's saying sort of how sorry he was for pushing about travelling with her. And she's saying it's okay. Then her mobile went. And while she's walking towards her office, she says something like ..." His face screwed in concentration trying to force the memory. "'Actually, I can't really talk at the moment, I'll ring you back in a while. But you'll never guess what I came back from Spain with!' Then after she finishes the call, this Tony asks her what it is she's come back with. I can't remember exactly the reply. But it's along the lines of 'My future, Tony baby! My future!' 'Which is what?' this Tony asks. 'Now that would be telling!' 'So tell. What?' 'Not a chance!' 'You and your fucking secrets, Davina!' Maybe not exactly those words. But that was the gist!"

"D'you know who she was talking to?" He shook his head. "Or what this thing was that she came back from Spain with?" But he didn't know that either. "How long was she there?"

"A week. Mister Miller's buried there. She stayed at the villa, a guest of his partner. Cleared up some paperwork and flew home. Didn't even unpack. Left her bags at her flat and came straight over to the office. She looked so tanned and lovely that day and then ..."

"Was she and this Tony an item?" He shook his head. "What about other boyfriends?"

"A Ricky something for a while. But I think he got dropped when Mister Carlin came on the scene."

"How did he take it?"

Robin shrugged.

"Who knows? Who likes being dumped, especially in favour of someone with money and wherewithal!"

"Have you had the police around?"

"Oh, yes. They wanted to know about any problems she may have had. Or disputes with people. Or anyone that might have wanted to harm her."

"And had she?"

"Not recently."

"Not recently?"

"She borrowed a large amount of money from some

individuals in Birmingham because she couldn't get the funding she needed for a project from her bank. There was a lot of problems, threats against her over what they thought they were due when the development sold."

"When was this?"

"Eighteen months, two years ago. It was quite a to-do at the time. But it all seemed to blow over."

"D'you tell the cops all this?"

"Oh, yes," he said, finishing his coffee. He slid a green square coaster towards him and made a point of placing cup and saucer precisely in the middle of it.

I gave him my card and asked him to ring me if he thought of anything else.

"She was twenty-seven," he said. "Had her whole life in front of her."

And now her future was behind her because she had something or knew something, or had unfinished business with someone.

CHAPTER 12

There were thick-looking clouds in a milky-grey sky and I guessed it wouldn't be long before it rained. There's something about autumn rain. Maybe it's because it prompts you into thinking you might be in for a real shit winter. I found myself rehearsing a few lines for Stafford as I walked to my car. The best lies have 70 per cent of truth in them. So it was just a case of being careful with the 30. He'd press me again about my visit to Davina. The lie would have to tie in with visiting Robin. Because it was as sure as apples grow on trees he'd tell Stafford I'd called. So it was going to have to be something convincing. I lit a fag. But got no inspiration from the nicotine. I was still struggling with a truthful-sounding lie when my mobile rang.

"Is that Eddie Sutton?"

"Who wants to know?"

"My name's Arnie. Steve give me your number. Said there might be a few quid in it for me."

"Maybe."

"You old bill?"

"Not any more."

"Said you might pay for some gossip." He coughed a real phlegmy smoker's cough.

"Maybe." There was silence which I guessed was while he spat out what he'd produced. "I'm after gossip on a particular subject. Perhaps we should meet."

"I'm going to Enfield dogs tonight," he said.

"Bit public, isn't it?"

He said there was some waste ground with skips behind the Tote booth. We arranged for 8 p.m.
"What d'you look like?" I asked.
"D'you know what George Clooney looks like?"
"Yes."
"Nothing like him."
"There's a surprise!"
"You'll know me when you see me."

I hadn't been to a greyhound meeting in years. I'd forgotten just how downmarket they were. Enfield was no exception. The stands, so-called, were a dozen wide concrete steps that circled the track from which the spectators viewed the races. At the top of the steps were a couple of bars and takeaway joints, all of them under an overhanging roof with fluorescent lighting fixed into it. The punters came in all shapes and sizes. Some drinking, some smoking or eating, usually chicken nuggets and chips smothered in ketchup from polystyrene boxes. Their wives or girlfriends, however pretty, always looked tarty.

The place was a mess from discarded betting slips, dog ends, dropped bottles. And all around there was noise. Noise, noise, noise. Bookmakers shouting, people shouting, people on phones. A solid wall of it occasionally transcended by a tannoyed monotone voice that sounded as though it had been trained at British Rail. The racetrack was flat and sandy, just wide enough to accommodate six greyhounds abreast of each other, bathed in hard, unremitting, fluorescent light. A voice announced the next race. The dogs were put in the traps and perhaps if the favourite had too much money on it, its balls were given a good hard twist to slow it. The lights dimmed. The electrically operated hare rounded the bend. The traps opened and the dogs in different-coloured striped jackets sprinted, panted and skidded round the circumference of the track. Someone behind me shrieked "Come on the five dog" as if the mutt could understand. It was over inside twenty seconds.

It occurred to me this was the other end of the Freemont spectrum. The punters there were rich, in evening wear, bejewelled, gambling for recreation. The punters here, mostly in trainers with shirts hanging out the back of jeans, gambled in order to make ends meet. Brompton Road to Enfield was about twenty miles. It could have been continents.

He was right. In all the hubbub he'd found an isolated spot. I guessed he was early thirties. He stood leaning against a wall, hands in the pockets of a long green gabardine army surplus jacket. He had long greasy hair that sat on its collar. He wore faded jeans, and black scuffed trainers.

"Eddie, yeah!" He was right about something else. He didn't look anything like George Clooney. He had a week's growth, stubby nose and pupils that didn't stop moving, and you could taste the tobacco on his breath. "My name's Arnald. But everyone calls me Arnie. Steve says you're all right."

"I need some info. There'd be a few quid in it for you. Heard of Tony Kreeger?"

"The Freemont Kreeger?"

I nodded, and asked if he'd heard anything about him recently.

"Not recent. The word is now Jack's back ..." and he pointed his thumb downwards.

"Meaning?"

"While Tony and Ronnie Miller was in charge there was a lot of drug business going on."

"I know, through Danny Carlin. What's the gossip on him these days?"

"As nasty a piece of work as ever," he said. The pupils kept moving as if he was trying to look everywhere at the same time. "Drugs mainly, loan sharking too. Like making a mint from property developing ain't enough." He touched a nostril with a nicotined index finger and sniffed a couple of times. "Goes to Newcastle a lot, I hear, and not for the football, if you know what I mean."

"I know he supplies in South London."

"Word is, he's got connections up there with the Grayston family."

He sniffed again, a different kind of sniff without the finger. The same kind as Ricky. He saw me looking and realised I understood. He offered me a fag and held a Zippo to his, then mine. He took a lungful and exhaled a stream of smoke into the remnants of daylight towards clouds of navy blue in a turquoise sky.

"Talking of the Freemont. Word is a Leon Doorrell is seriously after it," he said.

"Tell me about him."

"Algerian. Dark-skinned, with a stare that can put the shits up you! He publishes a couple of porn mags. *Strictly Discipline* and one called *Hot and Wet*, which is not about DIY plumbing though it does have a do-it-yourself side to it, I guess. Steve said this might be about him as well, so …" He pulled a magazine from an inside pocket and handed it to me. "Just to give you some idea. The real money comes from pussy. He runs a lot of girls from casinos and an internet dating site. Costs a few grand to join, for which you get a pin number to access photos and profiles of dozens of girls. You e-mail your choice. The message goes to an office of his. They page the girl with your name and number."

I took a lungful of tobacco myself, trying to decide if this was legit, speculation or just gob.

"Why page them?"

"Hard to trace a pager. The girl rings from a public telephone, fixes a meet. Cash up front."

"Nice work if you can get it."

"Two to three hundred quid a time. Four, five times a day. Maybe six days a week. Twenty-odd girls in his stable. I should say it's nice work! I'll save you the mental arithmetic, Mister Sutton. You're talking ten to twelve million quid a year."

I understood now why Doorrell would want the Freemont.

"And all good-looking, high-class pussy," he went on. "No dogs, no scrubbers. He has a lot of the what d'you call them, concierges of West End Hotels on his payroll and cops on vice to look the other way."

"What about the girls?"

"What about them?"

"How does he control them?"

"Once they start working for him, they're his property. They do what they're told, how they're told, when they're told. Or else!"

"Or else?"

"They're well paid. The ones that drive have expensive cars. And he lets them keep tips. But any trouble, sticking to money, unofficial tricks and they're history."

"History?"

"Gossip is" and he ran a finger across his throat.

"You're joking!"

"It's never been proved. But some of his girls do disappear. Turns out he has an older brother, Albert, who owns two undertaker businesses. One in Romford. One in Watford."

"You're pulling my leg, mate, right?"

"Do I look like I am?"

"But the cops must know!"

"Most of the girls are foreign. None pay tax or national insurance because all the tricks are for cash. So how you gonna prove that someone who doesn't officially exist has disappeared without a corpse? As for the cops, some are paid not to care. It's just one tom less to worry about."

"You seem to know a lot about him, Arnald."

"Call me Arnie. I hate that name Arnald. It's so shit! Can you imagine calling a baby Arnald. No wonder I got a habit!"

"How d'you know all this?"

"Mate of mine used to drive for a couple of his girls. He'd overhear things."

"Used to?"

"He got pulled one night for drink-driving. Banned for twelve months. So that was the end of his chauffeuring career. It wasn't only losing the money that pissed him off but losing the perks as well, if you get my drift!"

"Let me know what you hear about Tony Kreeger."

"Will do!"

"In the meantime, there's a hundred quid in the programme." I put it on the wall beside him and walked off.

CHAPTER 13

There were two bars packed to the gunnels, and a takeaway that stank of chips. So I headed for the stadium's restaurant called The Winners Enclosure. I was within a few yards of it when Danny Carlin came out chatting to some guy. He saw me and stopped. He stood, hands sunk deep in the pockets of a long black leather coat. Nice, but not as nice as my three-quarter-length, bottle-green leather one. We eyed each other for a moment. He waited, I supposed, for me to walk around him. But I didn't.

"Trouble with this place," he said to his friend, "is they let anyone in these days."

I hadn't seen him for two or three years. But he hadn't changed that much. The face still long and muscular with a small, crescent-shaped scar at the corner of his mouth. There were a few more lines across the forehead. The hair was different. It used to be long and over the ears. Now it was full on top. But the sides were cropped to the temples.

I gripped a bunch of keys in my pocket in case he fancied some. I'm as good as anyone in a street fight. Keys are okay. Stick one in someone's eye. It tends to concentrate their minds about carrying on. His friend was tall and beefy with jet-black hair slicked back. Of course he'd weigh in. But I'd made up my mind Danny would get it first. He waited another moment and when he saw I wasn't moving, said,

"What d'you know. Detective Constable Sutton! Oh, it's not DC any more, is it! I forgot you was kicked out. Kicked out," he said to his friend, "for beating up an innocent suspect. And in a fucking nick as well. What are the filth coming to!"

"Surprised to see you here, Danny. I would have thought horses were more your thing. Sport of kings, and all that. Or is it queens. I forget." He smiled a false smile. He wasn't queer. But you could tell he didn't like the crack all the same.

"Got a couple of dogs running here tonight. That's what you're able to do when you've got dough, Sutton. Buy dogs, cars, jewellery, houses. Whatever takes your fancy."

"Talking of bitches. How's Collette?"

His friend took a step towards me. Danny put a hand on his chest and told him it would wait.

"She's fine. Want me to fix up a date?"

Collette Hammond was Danny's interrogator. He handed people, usually men, over to her when he wanted answers that a good beating couldn't produce. She'd been a theatre sister at a London teaching hospital before getting involved with him. She knew anatomy. She knew her work. That's to say, she knew how to hurt people.

"You and Collette can discuss old times," he continued. "You know she has her own inimitable way of chatting."

"A four-syllable word. Blimey! There's hope for you yet."

He started to say something when someone called to him. He waved, then nodded and shoulder charged me as he walked past. His mate stood there though looking me up and down. I supposed so that he'd recognise me if we met again. And then he spat on the ground just missing my shoes and followed Danny.

It was 8 p.m. The turquoise sky had turned inky black. I went into the restaurant. It was a large bright warm room with shiny cutlery laid out nicely on red linen tablecloths.

The far wall had huge windows providing a good view of the track, where silhouetted against the night sky by hard lights the dog handlers paraded the greyhounds for the next race. I looked at the menu but didn't order, just sat at the bar and had a Scotch, my head still full of Danny. He was connected because of Davina and Davina was connected to Tony. Too much for coincidence. But not proof of anything. You have to gather facts. They have to fit the evidence. That's what you're taught at police training. You can't allow yourself to make them reinforce preconceived notions. But you still couldn't get away from it; Danny was always bad news, wherever, whenever!

He was a kid from social care with a record for shoplifting, mugging and TDA. He'd become a builder. A good one. But the thieving continued. Somewhere along the way in his late twenties, he started dealing drugs and with a builders' crew that could throw their weight around, he strong-armed his way into seriously supplying in South London. His main opposition was Oscar Maneera, who controlled things south of the river. But opposition disappeared because Oscar disappeared three months after Danny started an affair with Oscar's wife, Julia, an ex-bunny that fucked like a rabbit. And so with money from building projects and money from drugs, he fashioned himself a nice little empire. No one knows how Collette came on the scene. Maybe she'd started as a customer. It certainly wasn't through romance. Because Collette bats for the other side. But once she proved that she could get information from men where a good beating couldn't, she was in. It occurred to me to maybe get Arnie to tail her in case she was holding Tony.

I had another Scotch and looked at the magazine Arnie had given me. A glossy, well-produced, soft porn top-shelf piece.

They came in all shapes and cup sizes. Sally, nineteen, facing the camera with an index finger seductively in her mouth. Who looked as though her tits had been in more hands than the loose change in my pockets had. Tara, twenty-one, looking slightly dazed as though she'd just been given more than the key to the door. I turned over. And there was Zoe, with a page to herself, in airline pilot's outfit complete with cap. Tunic unbuttoned flashing her boobs with a caption beneath reading 'I can take you to cloud nine'. She looked younger. The publication date was, May 2011. So she'd worked for Doorrell. I looked through the rest of all thirty-seven pages. Purely for research on Leon, you understand! Then put it back in my pocket.

A blonde down the bar who looked as though her head had been on more hotel pillows than a chocolate mint turned my way. She had a nice smile and wore no rings. I looked back, giving it plenty of teeth, and picking up the a menu decided to eat after all, when my mobile trilled.

"Eddie! It's Jack."

"What's up?"

"I've had an e-mail from the solicitors."

"And?"

"We can't talk on the phone. Come over."

"Now?"

"Yes."

"Can't it wait until tomorrow?"

"No, it can't. Why, what you doing that's so important?"

What was important was me getting started on my favourite pastime with help of a babe who was also looking at a menu and over at me between pages.

"I'm in a bar!"

"We got one here! 10 p.m." and he rang off.

I slammed the menu shut. Left a tenner under my glass and headed for the door, unable to bring myself to take another look at what I'd be missing which was a night in bed with a well-stacked woman who looked as though she knew her way around a bloke.

The exit to the car park was through two open iron gates just past a small soft drinks kiosk. I was just to one side of it and noticed Danny a little way off talking to someone whose back was towards me. The lights dimmed for the next race. But you could still make out the figures. Danny shaking his head. The other guy gesticulating. You could see the hands open-palmed as if he were pleading. Carlin poked him in the chest with a finger and said something. The guy ran a hand through his hair, nodded, then ran both through his hair. He turned and began walking away, head down, hands now in his trouser pockets. It took me a couple of seconds to realise I'd been watching Ricky Houston.

CHAPTER 14

I got to the Freemont just after 10 p.m. and parked in Brompton Road because the car park was full. They knew at reception I was coming and sent me straight up.

"I've printed it off. Here, take a look."

"Good evening, Jack!"

"Yeah, yeah, good evening."

He handed it to me. Cornell, Buchanan, Halliday's letter heading looked posh even when printed off from an e-mail. The wording is what you'd have expected from a £750 an hour firm of Finsbury Square briefs. That they acted in connection with the estate of the late Mr Ronald Miller. That Jack was a beneficiary and was invited to attend their offices Thursday the 11th inst at 11.30 a.m. together with his birth certificate, passport, three utility bills no more than three months old, the original letter he'd received from the Spanish solicitors and the hard copy of this letter that would be with him before Thursday.

"We'll need to make travelling arrangements," I said. "Maybe you, me and Terry in two cars." Then told him to put the ad in *The Times* for Thursday and Friday. "There's nothing more to do until then," peeved I'd come all the way over for just for this.

A phone rang on his desk.

"Yes, Maxine. I do want them. But there's someone with me. No. I'm sure he won't mind." He turned to me and said, "This will only take a moment."

"Sure."

"I was chatting to her," he said, pointing to the

receiver, "about Davina after you left the other day. I didn't realise they were friends."

"Really!"

"She bought a flat from her. Even got a personal welcome."

"What d'you know!"

There was a knock on the door.

"The figures you wanted, Jack," Maxine said, handing him a piece of A4 paper.

"You remember Eddie, don't you?"

"Of course!" and she offered me her hand.

"Nice to see you again, Ms Andrews."

"Maxine, please."

"Eddie was just here following up some stuff on Tony."

"I'll leave you to it then."

"Seems like I've ruined his evening."

She had the most amazing blue eyes. Once they focused on you it was hard to disengage. Mainly because you didn't want to.

"Oh, it was nothing!" I said. "Just catching up with a couple of friends," I looked down and realised I was still holding her hand.

"Really! It sounded as though I'd dragged you away from something." Jack cut in.

"Nothing important!"

"Well, the least I can do is stand you a few drinks downstairs. I'll ring the bar."

"It's okay," Maxine said. "I'm going to reception, I'll take him, and sign for a couple."

"Sort Terry out for Thursday morning, Jack. I'll ring you tomorrow to let you know how we're going to do it. Okay?"

I came out of his office and headed for the stairs.

"This way," she said. "We have a private lift. Much quicker."

She opened the gate and we stepped into the two-man carriage side by side, almost touching. I smelt Chanel on a neck that disappeared into the V of a nicely filled out white shirt that in turn disappeared into the waistband of a black fitted skirt. "Much quicker than the stairs." She half-turned and couldn't help but know I'd been looking at her. I thought she'd turn away. But she didn't.

My hope was the lift might get stuck. No such luck.

"You've heard about Davina Miller?" I said.

"Yes. Shocking! What an absolutely dreadful way to meet your end."

"I understand you were friends."

"Friends?" She looked at me quizzically. "Acquaintants. We exchanged hellos if we ran into each other here."

"Didn't you buy a flat from her. Even get a personal welcome."

"Gosh! Where d'you hear that from?"

"Jack."

"Personal welcome?" She scratched her head. Then said, "Oh, I know what you mean. No. There was trouble with a fitted wardrobe door. She happened to be upstairs in an unsold apartment with an estate agent at the time the carpenter was in my flat. So she came down to say hello and see if it was sorted."

"And was it?"

"Oh, yes."

"What was wrong?"

"With what?"

"The wardrobe door."

"Wrong hinges. Size is everything, didn't you know!"

The lift door opened. She waited for me to exit. I waited for her. We were face to face almost nose to nose. She put a hand on the gate as it started to close on us.

"After you. I'm old-fashioned, the sort of girl that always waits for the other person to make the first move!"

CHAPTER 15

She led me to the bar and asked what my poison was.

"Scotch and American, please."

"Miss Maxine?" the barman asked.

"St Clements for me." She replied.

"I've changed my mind. I'll have a St Clements too." I said.

"Coming right up!"

And it did in less than a minute. Which is what happens when the General Manager orders. I took out my wallet. She put her hand on mine.

"On the house, remember?" She told the barman she'd sign for it. He left the pad and ballpoint for her and went off to serve someone else. She pulled it over and scribbled her name on the ticket.

"Cheers!"

"Cheers! You didn't have to change your mind on my account."

"I wouldn't have if I didn't want to. D'you never drink alcohol?"

"No, never!"

I thought she said 'never' too earnestly.

"You on the wagon?"

"Not a lot gets past you, Sutton, does it?"

"You remembered my surname."

"I wouldn't have if I didn't want to. I was a prisoner of it for a few years. But not any more. And I'm not going back behind bars." She smiled, put her hand on mine again and said, "Pardon the pun." She took a sip and licked her lips and I thought how nice it would be to lick them too. "Sorry if I came over a bit strong the other evening. I tend to be a bit frosty with people until I know them better."

"Still frosty?"

"Thawing! What's happening about you know who?"

"I have a few leads. He's safe for the next few days. At least … Don't look around yet," I said. "Not yet. But there's a guy over there sitting underneath the gold clock. Is he a regular?"

He was black and thin. And given he was sitting, I guessed about six foot. He had long frizzy hair like unravelled black two-ply sisal string, wide lips, a broad nose and large round eyes. He wore a creased evening suit and a skinny black tie knotted into an unbuttoned collar.

"Why d'you want to know?" she asked.

"He keeps looking my way. Then pretending he's not."

She slipped off her shoe, got off the stool to put it back on and copped a look.

"I've not seen him here before. Want me to check on membership? There'll be a photo."

"Thanks."

She cradled her chin in her hand. It was a curious pose. As if she were expecting to hear something outrageously important. Or just curious about you.

"Gosh! What cloak and dagger! So, how does someone end up a private detective?"

Buried memories and images floated to the surface like shaken sediment from meeting Danny. His so-called innocent suspect was a piece of rubbish named Joey Farmer, whose speciality was befriending au pairs newly arrived in England, getting them hooked on dope then pimping them. One had died from septicaemia; that's why I was interviewing him. We were in a small CID interview room in Mile Lane nick in the East End. Night-time. Joey sat legs outstretched, putting on a front as if he'd not a care in the world. We'd started at 8p.m. Two hours later he was still denying everything and taking the piss with smart-arse answers and a permanent smile across his rodent-looking face. Suspects lying is par for the course. Taking the piss is something else!

"You can't do nothing, and you know it, Sutton," he kept saying. "'Cause I got nothing to do with any little tart's death," he added, stabbing a finger across the desk at me.

A picture of a girl unconnected to Farmer popped into my head. My niece, Nicola. Eighteen, dead from a drugs overdose shot between her toes because she hadn't any other viable veins left. Just lying on a divan in her uni halls of residence with dried vomit on her blue T-shirt. I try very hard to hang onto my temper. I want to give Joey a slap or two. Or three.

"Nothing. You hear me?" And he spells out the word N-O-T-H-I-N-G.

"You're rubbish, Joey. I'm going to put you ..."

"N-O-T-H-I-N-G!"

"You'll be an old man when you come out."

"N-O-T-H-I-N-G!"

"That's if you ever come out."

"N-O-T-H-I-N-G!"

I looked at my watch.

"Interview terminated at 10.14 p.m."

I switched off the tape and something snapped. I pulled him up by his shirt front so he was halfway out of his chair and hit him with a left hook. A beauty right from the shoulder. The look on his face as he went over backwards was of complete and absolute surprise. When he landed, his mouth was bleeding. I bent down and grabbed him up. The blows rained in, even though the other DC with me was trying to pull me away. Joey's face turned red. His nose exploded with blood. The room filled with him shouting, then the alarm. I couldn't understand what he was saying. All I could see were the lips spurting blood where before they'd spurted ridicule. And his nose looking broken and gushing blood. And then the custody sergeant and two PCs were on top of me, pulling me away but not before I'd kicked him in the bollocks. He went down on his knees, was there a second or two holding his crotch, then he slumped backwards, spreadeagled, eyes closed, blood everywhere, face, shirt, jacket, trousers, even over his nice black leather shoes. His body heaved as he took in air. But he didn't know too much about it. I made an attempt to stomp on him. But three pairs of hands restraining me were too much.

I told her it was a long story. One that maybe I could tell her about over dinner some time, and asked her for her number.

"Is there a Mrs Private Detective?"

"No."

"Divorced?"

"Never been married."

She raised an eyebrow.

"How come?"

"Far too young."

"Or maybe you just haven't met the right woman."

"Possibly!"

She picked up a paper serviette off the bar and blotted her lips on it. Then picked up the barman's ballpoint and scribbled her number across her lipstick imprint. I folded the serviette carefully and put it in my pocket and said I'd be in touch. She held my stare and said in touch was good. And then she headed out of the bar to reception. She had a nice walk, nice legs, nice bum, easy on the eye. Easy on this eye anyway. She was nearly at the exit when she looked over her shoulder to find we were staring at each other. I finished my drink and headed for the door casually looking around. But the black guy had gone.

It was nearly midnight when I left the Freemont. It had been raining. The traffic lights were reflected in the puddles, red and red amber in zigzagged shapes, while the blues and pinks and whites of shop lights were cast over the soaked pavements. I got to my Beema, which I'd parked by the high pavement to find the black guy who'd been clocking me from under the clock in the Freemont leaning against my car.

"This in your way?" I asked.

"It's Eddie Sutton, right?"

"Eddie's my twin brother. We're always being mistaken for each other."

"You don't think I've been hanging around all evening by accident, do you? A friend who works in the casino phoned to say you'd turned up. And besides, my mate over there knows your boat 'cause you did him once."

I looked across the road. There was a Chelsea tractor parked by the kerb underneath the yellow street lights. But too far for me to see the face.

"What you doing for Jack then, Mister Private Eye? That's what I want to know."

"We're just good friends!"

"Really!"

"Yeah, really! Would I lie to you?"

"You know you don't make a very good first impression."

"It's what they kept telling me at Rampton. And Broadmoor."

"Well, whatever you're doing for him, my boss, Mister Doorrell, would like you to hand in your notice."

"Really!"

"Yeah, really."

"Why?"

"He didn't give a reason. He's not a reason-giving sort of person regarding his decisions. There's just one redundancy item."

"What's that?"

"A promise not to break both your legs."

"How generous. But I've sort of committed myself."

He took the last drag on his fag and flicked it away. It was carried along by the rainwater then disappeared down a drain. He lit another, then took a few steps towards me. The face in the Chelsea got out and leaned against the door.

"Well, my advice to you, Mister Sutton, would be to get uncommitted before something nasty happens to you and you can't work, committed or not." He ran a finger and thumb down my lapel. I'd already fisted my car keys, waiting my moment to use them. Another second or two and he'd get the full Beema experience. That's to say, a BMW car key in the eye. "Mister Doorrell said no violence. So no violence it is. But that's only on today's market. Mister Doorrell is not the sort of person that takes no for an answer, if you get my drift."

"Your drift is crystal clear."

"Good. Otherwise it's likely we'll be bumping into each other again." And before I could stop him, he'd crushed his cigarette out on the Beema's roof and walked off to his mate.

CHAPTER 16

The WPC at the front desk jotted down my name on a piece of paper and asked if that was Sutton with one t or two, then dialled Stafford's extension, gave him my name, then asked me if I'd wait in an interview room across the hall. It was stark and anonymous. High windows, bluey-grey painted walls, plain wooden desk, padded wooden chairs. Just like the rooms at Mile Lane nick. I remembered the next day after I'd beaten Joey up. I sat waiting in the same interview room where it had happened. Some of the lads I passed on the way in smiled and winked as if to say 'Shame you didn't kill the scroat', others wouldn't even look at me. The door opened. It was the Chief Inspector and a sergeant from CID. I stood to attention. He looked me up and down and asked if I knew why they were there. And without waiting for an answer said, 'It's to do with last night's incident.' He ran over the facts, of course omitting that he'd loved to have done the same thing, probably, to all the villainous bastards he'd interviewed in his time. Cautioned me. Took my warrant card, then suspended me from duty. He asked if I wanted to make a statement. But I knew better than to even open my mouth to take a breath.

It all felt a bit dreamlike as though it wasn't really happening. 'You should have known better, Sutton. What the hell did you think you were doing?' he said as I got to the door. But I got the impression that was for the benefit for the sergeant beside him. They all had their say. The Area Commander with his small pinched face and his tunic so square on his shoulders you'd think he still had the hanger in it. 'For heaven's sake, man, and you a DC.' Sympathetic? Understanding? What do you think! The Department for Professional Standards looked at it. Then the CPS, and they decided to prosecute.

The magistrates' court was small. I looked around for familiar faces. But there weren't any. The solicitors' well was unusually crowded. The long public benches behind the grill also full, as if the word had got around and they were wanting to see a copper get it for once. I looked at the magistrates. I knew the middle face. I'd given evidence before it a long time ago. Forbes something double-barrelled. He looked me up and down over bifocals, withdrew a handkerchief from his jacket sleeve and blew his nose. The Clerk of the Court beneath him drew his attention to some papers. He turned from me to him, gave him a tight little smile. Then sat back in his seat, one manicured hand on top of the other.

Assault Occasioning Actual Bodily Harm, contrary to section 47 of the Offences against the Person Act 1861. People stared at me as the clerk read the charge and asked for my plea. It felt more like being in a cage than a dock. The eyes switched to the bench. Joey was called, his injuries healed by then. Though if I'd had my way there would have been an action replay. He looked solemn but you could tell underneath loving every minute of it. Then the other DC. Then Robins, the custody sergeant, hair greased, uniform looking almost starched. Then the two PCs. I watched Forbes something during the giving of evidence. He picked an ear, looked at the wax, then flicked it away. It lasted less than twenty minutes. He consulted his notes, consulted the clerk, then his colleagues either side, then asked if I had anything to say. 'No, nothing, your honour.' Because there was nothing more to say. And because my brief had said what he could. I got six months, suspended for two years.

I knew I was out even before appearing in front of the three of them, the Commander and the two superintendents, all sitting there in a line like three monkeys. My Federation brief gave it his best shot, but he might as well not have bothered. They adjourned for half an hour, then returned. I only remember the one phrase from everything said. 'You are required to resign.'

Steve and a few other colleagues who dared to make contact with me wondered how I'd earn a living. Security work? The idea lasted a day. Professional debt collecting? That idea lasted less than a day. In the end I decided to stick with what I knew best and got a job with a firm of enquiry agents, Hatchman and Lewis. 'Honesty, Discretion, and Expertise that cannot be equalled.' Established 1994 by a pair of wide boys as iffy as the people they investigated. I was with them for a year, then struck out on my own. And that's how it started — from a shitty little back room in an office block off Stratford Broadway in East London. Four years later I'm in a half-a-million-pound flat, earning three times as much as I would have as a DC. I shop for my clothes in the West End and my groceries and stuff in Camden, the place for the nouveau upwardly mobile where you can buy anything from a bible to a dildo.

I sat there waiting for Stafford for maybe ten minutes. And then in he bowled. I was about to stand through force of habit, which is the protocol when a senior officer enters a room. Fuck it! No automatic about it now. Maybe that was a measure of how the whole episode and that part of my life were behind me. He plonked himself in a chair opposite, dropped a yellow A4 pad on the desk and said,

"Once upon a time. There was a girl called Davina Miller who was murdered because … It's your turn, Eddie. How does the story continue?"

"Not with everyone lived happily ever after."

"Just the middle and the end will do."

I didn't like the idea of lying to him. But there was no alternative. Besides, there was a part of him that wasn't expecting the truth anyway.

"Ronnie owed Danny Carlin some money for drugs. Ronnie couldn't or wouldn't pay. Then Ronnie dies and my guess is Danny, who is already in business with Davina, puts the bite on her." The thing about me is, once I start spinning a story, after a while it all sounds plausible even if it's all a load of crap.

"So you think he killed her trying to find out where Ronnie's money might be?"

"Yes." Then I thought, who knows? Maybe he did. They had a successful business and were making a shedload of money. And a 100 per cent of something is always better than 50. I've known people kill for less. And the idea of Danny getting twenty-five years sent a warm feeling right through me. As warm as if Stafford had told me Carlin had been hit by a bus and wasn't expected to survive the day.

"What kind of money?"

"What?"

"What kind of money?"

"Don't know!"

"You ever heard of Charles Dickens?

"Yes."

"I thought you might. 'Cause he used to make up stories as well. So how did you get involved with Davina and Carlin, then?"

"She hired me to see if I could find where Ronnie's money is. Because there's very little in Spain."

He slammed his ballpoint down on his pad.

"One half of me thinks you're lying."

"And the other half?"

He leaned over the desk so that he was inches from me.

"Knows you're fucking lying. The bit about Danny is good. Because we know he's a serious player in South London. But I don't buy the rest." He sat back in his chair and said, "You know what! I'll order some coffee while you think of a better story." He twisted his head round the door and asked someone if they could get some. "D'you take milk?"

"Full cream, lots of cholesterol."

"That's a yes then!"

We sat with the coffees between us, Stafford just staring at me.

"Well?"

"Well what."

"Do I hear a further bid than you were helping Davina?"

"'Fraid not!"

"We went through Davina's e-mails and phone messages."

"And?"

"She had two calls from someone called Tony the day she died. The first one said he wanted to speak to her because he'd phoned Spain and been told she'd come back with stuff and he wanted to know what she had. D'you know anyone called Tony?"

"My barber. His name's Tony. What did the other message say?"

"Why are you interested, if you don't know anyone called Tony?"

"It might be connected with some other business of mine."

"Such as?"

"Some dealing."

"So, where was I?" Stafford continued. "Oh, yes! I know. Someone called Tony. He's got a dad."

"That's nice. I'm a great believer in families."

"His dad's name is Jack Kreeger. Who happens to have been a business partner of Ronnie Miller."

"What d'you know!"

"You seen him lately?"

"How would I? I don't know anyone called Tony."

"Except your barber."

He told me that in the other message Tony said he wanted to speak to her. He was coming round and if she didn't answer the door to him, he'd kick it in.

"And now," Stafford added, "Tony Kreeger's nowhere around. Funny that! If CCTV catches him around Davina's, I understand he drives a red Ferrari, coupled with the fact he's done the Indian rope trick, … Well, you can see where this could lead."

"Where?"

"The Old Bailey." This other business of yours. What's that about?"

"I'd need a favour."

"Oh, really? Such as?"

"To know if a couple of people have form."

"And you want me to find out on the basis of – what? You having been so helpful?" Stafford thought it over as he scratched his head and said, "Okay, Eddie. Tell you what! As I've known you a while and I like you. Seriously I do. And as you've marked my card on lots of occasions for which I've been grateful, I'll help you on the basis that you phone me tomorrow and tell me that your memory's come back. Names?"

"Doreen Entwhistle. Aka Zoe Fontaine – and Maxine Andrews."

He scribbled them on the pad. He lay back in his chair

looking at me over the rim of his cup.

"Going back to Davina. We're not talking about a bit of snotty-nosed villainy, Eddie. We're talking murder, or worst way manslaughter of a 27-year-old woman in a not very pleasant way. She must have suffered a great deal of pain. So think on that. Or you and I are going to fall out."

I decided Stafford needed a sweetener.

"I've heard a bit of gossip that might help you. She had some aggro with people in Birmingham over money. Might be something. Might be nothing. I also hear a whisper Danny goes to Newcastle a lot and meets with the Grayston family. Might be where his gear's coming from."

"Where d'you hear it?"

"On the grapevine."

"And the name of this grapevine?"

"Just the grapevine."

I didn't finish my coffee. I buttoned my jacket and told him I'd see if there was any more stuff doing the rounds. Then drove back to my office.

CHAPTER 17

I'd only been back a few minutes. Had hardly started listening to my messages when the entryphone went. Someone had their finger on it and wasn't going to take it off until I answered. The someone was Zoe. She was wearing black jeans, black shirt, under a black leather jacket. No make-up. No cute hair style, just the lot pushed back. She stood in the middle of the office, arms clutched around her, hugging herself so tightly that bunches of her jacket gathered in tight folds under her arms.

"You don't look at all well. What's the matter?" I said.

"I didn't know where to go or what to do. Then I thought of you. I'm so frightened." I offered her a chair. "I got abducted."

"Must be something in the water!"

"It's not funny. It's not funny at all."

She rummaged in her shoulder bag for some cigarettes. Lit up and then asked if I minded her smoking. I said 'no' and she tossed the pack across my desk.

"I was walking up Greencroft to my car last night when a motor pulled up beside me. A couple of guys grabbed me, bundled me into their boot and took off. I was so shit scared I can't tell you."

"Where did they take you?"

"Not sure. Local. I was only in there for fifteen minutes max."

"What happened? You escape?"

"Do I look like Wonder Woman!"

"Listen. Don't give me any attitude. You came here uninvited."

"Sorry!" She kept flicking non-existent ash into an ashtray. Then started walking around the office. Around and around. "They let me out a few hours ago. Just dumped me outside my flat. Threw my bag and shoes out the car and took off."

"Same guys?"

She shrugged.

"I think so."

"What did they want?"

She sat down and burst out crying. The tears streamed down the sides of her face over her lips and rolled into the corners of her mouth.

"Shit! I thought I was all cried out."

"What happened? They, they …?" I searched for a euphemism and could only think of "molest you?"

She tried to speak, but couldn't; she just shook her head instead.

"No." She closed her eyes and gathered herself. "They dragged me out by my hair, then pulled me through this courtyard into a small room without windows."

"Office? House?"

"Don't know. It was empty. Except for a beam running across it. And a desk with restraints at the end of it. One of the guys handcuffed me over the beam. Then they left. I heard voices, then a car engine. I was left there on my own for I don't know how long. I tried freeing myself, but couldn't. Then this woman came in."

I had a bad feeling about what was coming next. I asked her what the woman looked like. But I already knew.

"Tall, maybe six foot. Bony face, beakish nose, schoolmarmish, red hair combed back in a pleat. My head was pounding. My heart too. I said I didn't know what she wanted. I didn't have any money. She just stood there looking at me. Silent. Just looking, arms folded, smiling, just looking at me from head to foot."

Zoe closed her eyes, wiped her face with the back of her hand. But more tears came, leaving a streak on her cheeks.

"D'you want a drink? Tea, coffee?"

"Make that a Scotch." I fixed her one. She downed it in two. Then held out the glass.

"You don't have to go on."

"I do. Because there's stuff I should have told you the other day. Now I'm shit scared of what might happen to me. She kept looking, this woman. Then said, 'First, it's clothes off.' The way she said it, so matter of fact, it sent a chill through me. 'I think you'll look really yummy naked.' She ran a hand across my boobs and then she stripped me. I tried again pulling at the beam. But it wouldn't give. The cuffs just cut into my wrists. She put a finger across my lips, tutted, then slapped me across the face a couple of times. She must have had scissors because what she couldn't remove, shirt, bra, she cut. I started sweating. I tell you, I've never been so scared in my life."

I got a mental image of Zoe handcuffed stark naked around a beam and had a Scotch myself. I'm sure what had happened had been traumatic. But I could tell she could see the recounting was stirring my juices, and in a perverse way even with the upset she was getting off on the effect it was having on me.

"She came up behind me and cupped my breasts in her hands, said something about me having a nice body and that I smelt great. Then she asks me if I like girls. I shook my head and said, 'Not like that.' I just about got the words out because my voice cracked and I started crying. 'I do,' she says. 'I like them a lot. Best of all when I'm having them doing what they're told.' Then she began stroking my hair and I could feel her putting strands of it to her face. I asked what she wanted. I was now near to hysteria. I kept asking and asking. Finally she says, 'We're going to have a question and answer session.' She came round to face me and said, 'You sure you don't like girls? You've got such a nice body.' She ran her fingers across my forehead. 'It's funny they always sweat once I have them undressed. I suppose it's because they don't know what I'm going to do to them. Their eyes dilate to the size of marbles like yours have. You can smell the fear on them. It rolls down their faces and between their breasts' and she moved a finger down my face and between my boobs. 'And then they sweat from the armpits and it runs down their bodies' and she traced a finger from my armpit to my navel. 'It's pure fear.' And she was right. I was sweating and so scared it's a wonder I didn't crap over her shoes. Then she rolls up her shirtsleeves and takes a cane hanging beside the desk and just leaves it full view of me and my guts wrenched in a knot so badly I thought I was going to throw up. She said she wanted some information and if I didn't give it to her or if she thought I was lying, she'd hurt me. I told her I'd tell her whatever she wanted to know."

She finished the Scotch, closed her eyes and took some deep breaths. I was about to ask what happened when she said,
"This fucking lunatic bitch then starts on about how she knows how to hurt people. And how she's really good at it. How she's had men in this room she says who have cried, begging for the pain to stop. All sorts; 30-year-olds, 40-year-olds, tearaways that think they're the next Al Capone. 'I like them young,' she says to me. 'Being stripped and humiliated by a woman like that stays with them for ever. But

regardless of age, the pain doesn't stop, Zoe,' she says. 'Not until they've told me everything I want to know. But then men are easy to get information from once you have them hanging by their ankles and spread their legs. So, Zoe …' She keeps calling me Zoe like we're the best of fucking friends! 'So, Zoe. Let's make a start. I suggest you tell me everything I ask. Otherwise, you see the desk. I'm going to put you over it with your wrists secured in those restraints and then when I've got you nicely spread across it, cane you until I've taken every piece of skin off your nice little backside and then if necessary every piece of skin off the back of your thighs. You can yell and shout as much as you like. That's okay. Because the room's soundproofed.' 'Don't. Please don't,' I screamed. 'I'll tell you whatever you want to know. I'll tell you.'"

Zoe sat there, then let out a long low breath. And so did I. I had a mental image of her spread across a table taking stroke after stroke from a cane across her cute pink little arse and it's a wonder my fly zip didn't split from the pressure against it.

"So what did Collette want?"

"You know her? You know that fucking psycho?"

"Oh, yeah! Her name's Collette Hammond. She's an interrogator for Danny Carlin. Her forte's men. She has them delivered to her handcuffed hands behind their backs, hangs them up by their ankles, strips them, spreads their legs and attaches electrodes to their testicles. Her other trick is to tie a piece of string around the scrotum to cut off the blood supply. Either way inside ten minutes they tell her everything she wants to know. Maybe less, because she enjoys what she does. And does it hardly leaving a mark. She once told a contact of mine what really turns her on is when men start whimpering."

Zoe slumped back in her chair and held her hand to her forehead.

"Jesus Christ! What have I got myself into!" Then she looked up at me as though something had just crossed her mind and with the hint of a smirk said, "How d'you know all this? Don't tell me she's had your trousers down."

"I tried nailing her for three years when I was a DC at Mile Lane."

"And?"

"Never even got close. So what did she want?"

"It's a long story."

I tipped a little more Scotch into her glass and a splash into mine and told her she had the floor.

"While Jack was away Ronnie, to begin with, but then later Tony mostly was supplying at the Freemont from Danny Carlin, who was introduced to him by a woman called Davina Miller, Ronnie's daughter. Then Tony got a chance to do a real big deal with some Russians. Because he doesn't see a great future at the Freemont. What with Jack coming back and this Maxine bitch straightening the place out and looking like a permanent feature. So he's looking for a new career."

"And a drug dealer's one of them, is it?"

"He didn't have all the dough to purchase. So Danny supplied him with £350,000 worth of product."

"Which was?"

"Cocaine. The deal was, Tony could sell it to the Russians for half a mil. They in turn would cut it and start dealing it. Tony gives Danny back the £350,000 plus twenty grand for fronting the gear. Everybody would be happy."

"I feel there's a but coming!"

"A big one. Tony got the stuff. But the next day on the way to pick up some guys to meet the Russians with, he got carjacked. So now no gear, no money."

It was the oldest scam in the book. The Russians would have been friends of Danny's and the carjackers his employees. And all things being equal, which they probably were, Davina the one setting Tony up with Carlin in the first place. And Tony had fallen for it all.

She took a swig of the Scotch, rocked the remains around the glass and finished the lot.

"Then," she continued, "Danny starts putting the squeeze on Tony. Dope or dough. He was at his wits' end because Danny's got a reputation. Then Danny says there's a way out. He'll send his people to gamble at the Freemont on the tables where Tony's the pit boss. They win five, six grand a time over six months until the winnings reach half a mil. Debt cleared."

"And presumable Tony roped you and Ricky in to help?" She nodded. "So?"

"Carlin recorded the conversation. Then after a month or so of winnings he threatened to tell Jack, who was back by then, unless Tony turned it into a permanent arrangement and turned a blind eye to Danny's people supplying some of the really rich clients with gear."

I took a fag from her packet and lit up, blew a plume of smoke at the ceiling. She brushed the last of her tears away. Bit her lip and said,

"It gets worse!"

"How much worse can it get?"

"On a scale of one to ten? Eleven! Tony decided to do something about things. Ricky has a friend, Lenny Jordan. A thief Ricky tells me you met at his flat who you've nicked a few times who's a bit handy with safes. So Tony hired him to break into Carlin's offices and steal the CD recording. He pinched some other stuff, a watch, some cash, some gear, just to make it look random."

I knew what was coming. It was so obvious. I couldn't think how Tony couldn't have anticipated it. For someone who wanted to be a drug dealer, he sounded a real dope. If you'll pardon the pun!

"You know what I'm going to say, don't you?" she said.

"Jordan played the CD, realised what he had and started blackmailing Tony."

"Not quite. He said he wanted an extra twenty grand for it. Or he'd tell Jack."

"Did you tell Collette all this?"

She nodded and pulled the sides of her jacket together even though the office was warm. No arrogant airline pilot's pose now. Just a frightened little wanna-be.

"She'd have had me across that desk if I hadn't told her."

"You can make book on it. She likes hurting people. She likes it a lot. To the point of videoing it for her and her girlfriend's home entertainment. She ask you where Jordan lived?"

Zoe tried to speak, but couldn't for the moment. Then she said,

"Yes. I knew the name of the flats and its whereabouts. Because Tony had me wait in the car once on the way to dinner while he stopped off for a word. But not the actual flat."

I took the address as far as she knew it from her.

"D'you have his phone number?" She shook her head. And said she could get it from Ricky. "Ring him."

She pulled her mobile out, scrolled and rang.

"Why d'you need it?"

"Jordan has to be warned. They'll be looking for him to get the CD because it incriminates Carlin. It's evidence he's a drug dealer, and that he was proposing to commit theft and embezzlement from a legally licensed casino. And also that once Collette's finished with him, Danny'll break both his legs by way of a message to others." And then it suddenly occurred to me who'd searched Tony's flat and what they'd been looking for.

She pulled out a fag, tried to light up with a Zippo. But her hand shook so much she couldn't manage it.

"Voicemail."

"Leave a message. Did Collette mention Tony?"

"Only something about hoping to have an opportunity of reprimanding him."

Which meant Danny didn't have him. But then I already knew that. Because if he did, there would have been no need to abduct Zoe. So the focus now swung on this Leon Doorrell character. But it seemed to me there were bits of this puzzle missing. No, not missing. Didn't fit!

Zoe started crying again. She had her head in her hands and was giving it plenty of welly.

"My poor Tony! Can you imagine what that perverted fucking cow could do to him?"

I told her Danny wouldn't hand him over, because Tony was an investment. She looked up; there were tears on her cheeks slowly meandering down her face. I handed her a tissue. She wiped her eyes, then blew her nose. A real snotty fill-up-a-tissue job.

"You reckon?" she said.

"Collette mention anything besides the CD?" Zoe gave me a curious look. "A book maybe?"

"Why would she? Jordan pinched a CD."

"Just wondered."

"What kind of a book?"

"Tony ever mention a book?"

She forced a smile.

"Tony? The last book he read I reckon was Jack & Jill. He doesn't do books. Why? Is she after a particular book?"

"It doesn't matter. Tony ever mention that Davina

might have set him up with Carlin and that the deal with the Russians, was just a sting to get Danny back in to the Freemont?"

"Jesus! No! Why, did she?"

"Tony, Davina, Carlin, the Freemont. How's your maths?"

"My maths?"

"Two and two mean anything to you?"

Her jaw dropped.

"You know that never occurred to me."

"What happened after Collette finished questioning you?"

"She made herself a drink at the other end of the room. Came back and just stood staring at me, mug in hand, like I was the fucking biscuit with her tea or coffee."

"She say or do anything?"

"She brushed the hair out of my eyes and said it had been a good chat. Then pulled a mobile and left a message saying she'd got the information she needed and to ring her back. Then dialled again and said she was finished and wanted to know how long. Then maybe ten, fifteen minutes later unlocked the handcuffs and told me to get dressed."

She tried lighting a cigarette and this time succeeded.

"The sick bitch told me to leave my panties," she exclaimed through a bluey-grey stream of smoke that rose but dissipated before it got to the ceiling. "Can you believe that! Then these guys turned up, dragged me back into the boot and dumped me outside my flat. Threw my bag and shoes out the car and took off."

"I don't suppose you got a registration?" She pulled a face and I felt stupid for asking. "When was this?"

"Eight-ish this morning. I must have been there longer than I thought." She told me that she had been in such a state. She'd showered, then bathed and still felt dirty. Made herself breakfast. But couldn't eat. Tried to get some rest. Couldn't and decided to come round here.

"Why?"

"Why what?"

"Come here."

"For some advice about what to do."

"Why do anything? Collette's got what she wanted."

"D'you think I should disappear for a while, in case she has me grabbed again?"

"Why would she?"

She shrugged and said,

"Maybe the psycho's taken a fancy to me." She pretended to spit and added, "Fucking dyke bitch!"

"They abducted you because they couldn't find Tony. I reckon you're safe. Go home, take a sleeping pill. Get some kip."

"But what if …?"

"You'll be all right."

"You sure? I don't know how to thank you for listening."

"You sure you don't know Jordan's flat number?"

"No. Why?"

"I'm going to pay him a visit. With a bit of luck he's still breathing."

"But you don't know the flat!"

"I have the block and its location. Maybe twenty quid will help someone's memory regarding the number."

She studied me for a moment across the desk. Then asked how I had the stomach for all this kind of aggro.

"It's a gift!"

"Better you than me."

We came downstairs. Her car, a bright red Mazda MX5 sports, had a parking ticket. She snatched it off the windscreen and said,

"Ever had that feeling, it's just not going to be your fucking day"!

CHAPTER 18

Trent House in Witley Street was a council estate at the Elephant and Castle. It was 1930s with long walkways that ran the length of the block, overlooking a concrete courtyard with notices NO BALL GAMES, NO CYCLING posted at three or four spots. Many of the front doors had locked gates across them even on the first- and second-floor levels.

A minute later and I would have missed it. A white van with Acme Builders painted on its side with the back doors open and two guys in ski masks grabbing hold of Lenny Jordan. One held his collar and arm while the other dragged him by his other arm. I screeched up beside them and kicked one hard in the shin. He let go of Jordan and went to the cab, presumably for a baseball bat or something as useful. But I slid the door shut on him trapping his fingers in it. His howl reverberated around the empty courtyard, bouncing from brickwork to brickwork with a hollow tiny echo.

"The fucker's done me, Dell!" he shrieked. "Help me! Help me!" He tried opening the door with his free hand but couldn't reach. "Help me," he screamed, as blood dripped down the van's white paintwork like strawberry sauce down ice cream.

Dell let go of Jordan, took a step or two towards me, changed his mind, opened the door, helped his mate in and took off, leaving the smell of burnt rubber wafting up from the road.

I turned to look for Lenny and he hit me on the side of the head with a brick. I went down on my knees, then sprawled. Not unconscious. But not with it. There was new blood now.

Mine. From my temple meandering down the side of my jaw. I propped myself against a wall, feeling the salty taste creeping into my mouth. I pressed the wound with a handkerchief. I wanted to close my eyes. But knew if I did I'd pass out. I splashed some water on my face from a puddle. It helped a bit. Then I struggled to my feet.

"You all right, lad?"

I looked up; there was an old dear in a hairnet looking over the walk-way.

"I'll live. Did you see which way he went? The guy that hit me?"

"Out into the main road."

"I'm looking for a Lenny Jordan. Do you know what flat number he is?"

"Can't help you, love!" and she closed her front door.

I took some deep breaths to gather myself , then started half-walking, half-stumbling around the courtyard looking for him in case she'd just given me a bum steer, though I knew realistically he'd gone. I looked under a few cars neatly parked within the white lines of their bays. Behind an open metal-fronted shelter for wheelie bins. Nothing. I even looked inside a couple.

I sat in my car and took a belt from a hip flask from the glove compartment. There was just under a quarter of a bottle, I finished the lot. I looked at the wound in the driver's mirror. There was a gash at the hairline. Red, swollen, but no longer bleeding But the blood had matted in my hair. I went home and had a proper drink, bathed the wound, put a plaster over it and lay on my bed. I closed my eyes and let the images, the van, the screaming, the blood, float in front of me. Chances were Dell's mate had lost a couple of fingers. Served him right! And Jordan? He didn't know how lucky he'd been. And my thanks? Being clouted with a brick!

CHAPTER 19

The liquor, the injury and the sheer trauma of the episode took its toll. I drifted off and stayed drifted until the following morning, which started with a call from Jack who told me he'd had a call from 'you know who!' Who'd given him a dozen seconds with Tony. I told him to be careful about what he said on the phone. Then asked if he was sure it was Tony.

"Yes, of course!"

"What did he say?"

"To help him."

"Did you record it?"

"No time."

"Shame."

"Well, at least I know he's ... well, you know. It's something, Eddie, believe me! It sort of helps. It's some relief to know ... you know."

" Sure! I understand .Where did you take the call?"

"Here at home."

"Mobile or landline?"

"Landline."

I told him it was as well he'd rung, and if he hadn't I would have rung him because I needed to speak to him. So we made a meet for 11a.m. at the Freemont

He was sitting behind his desk. Bolt upright, one hand on top of the other, looking very corporate with horn-rimmed specs as if he were posing for a portrait. He said 'good morning'. The sun streamed in from the window behind him. The room was bright. He was not. He sounded tired. No. Exhausted, though it was first thing in the morning. I suppose it was from the stress of it all. He asked what had happened to my head. I turned profile and told him I'd had an argument with a cupboard door and the door had won. I could feel a lump under the plaster. It was still sore. But not as painful as it had been.

"I don't suppose you've heard from the kidnappers again?"

"No."

"Tony's why I wanted to speak to you. You're going to get heat from a copper called Stafford. He's building a case against Tony for Davina's death. He's got threatening voice messages to Davina from him. And there might be CCTV of Tony driving around that area, and if any of her neighbours remember him calling that day … Your Tony is in real hot water. My guess is that the Freemont's under surveillance and your telephone calls are being monitored. That's why I told you to be careful before about what you said."

"He's already been. Yesterday afternoon. He wanted to speak to Tony."

"What did you say?"

"The first thing that came into my head. He'd taken a few days off to visit a girlfriend in Bournemouth." He shrugged as if to say, what do expect with no time to think about an answer!

"Did he believe you?"

"Probably not. It's not that coppers are paranoid. They just think everyone's lying."

"They're not far wrong."

"I said I'd have Tony ring him as soon as he was back. He asked for the girl's address. I said I didn't even know her name, let alone where she lived." His phone rang. He said, "Yes. Tell them I said they can go fuck themselves," and slammed the receiver down. Then he said he wasn't able to sleep at night because of Tony. "It keeps gnawing at my insides," he said, clasping his head in his hands. "I can't tell you how badly. Where is he? How's he being treated? I can't sleep, I can't eat!" He inhaled heavily, short of breath and took a few shots from his inhaler. "And now I've got this Stafford geezer giving me grief!"

I told him things would be okay because they needed Tony alive. Then I asked him what else Stafford had said.

"He wanted to know when Tony had last seen Davina."

"What did you say?"

"How should I know! I'm only his father!" He took a tissue and mopped his brow, then wiped his glasses. "You sure Tony's all right?"

"He's safe at the moment. Did Stafford tell you that Tony rang Davina twice the day she died?"

"What about?"

"Drugs, probably."

"Naaa! Not my Tony. I know it went on while I was away. But that's all history."

"History has a habit of repeating itself. My guess is she was killed because of drugs or …"

"Or what?"

"Someone thought she had Ronnie's book."

"Jesus Christ! How does she come to be mixed up with that?"

"Ronnie was her father."

"But even so! No. You're wrong about Tony. You'll see!" he added.

I looked at him and was reminded of the old adage. That husbands and parents are the last to know! I told him what to do if Stafford came back. Which was to play it cool. He knew nothing.

"Don't give him Tony's mobile number." I doubted

they could trace him without a number. Though the chances were the SIM card had been removed anyway. "And if you get a visit from telephone engineers telling you that your lines need checking, they'll be from the Met. So tell them to come back next year. And then there's Maxine. Tell her she knows nothing about nothing. Period!"

He nodded. He finished wiping his specs and as he replaced them, told me he'd decided to go to Davina's funeral. I said I was surprised her body had been released so soon.

"The coroner was sympathetic to the fact that she was Jewish."

"What's Jewish got to do with it?"

"They bury the body as soon as possible. Tradition."

"Where?"

"Bushey. It's a Jewish cemetery on the outskirts of North West London."

"Who's organised it?"

"Sybil, her mother. And her brother and his wife."

"I may come along." He asked why. "There's nothing like a funeral to unearth things! There'll be faces there. Danny, Stafford, Ricky. Maybe even the person that murdered her. What d'you know about her brother?"

"His name's Norman. An accountant. Lives in Pinner where he also has offices. Married to a Scottish girl named Brenda."

My head started hurting again. He had someone bring coffee and aspirin. I hoped it would be the blonde with too many buttons undone. Because I liked looking at her. But it was a tall thin guy, who looked as though he could moonlight haunting houses.

"You look pensive, Eddie."

"You sure there's no one else with a motive for kidnap,

Jack?"

He poured us each a cup and slid mine towards me.

"If it was just for money, any one of a half-dozen faces. But there's only two that would know about the book."

"What about Terry?"

"No way! Why d'you ask?"

"Because it isn't Danny."

"How d'you know?"

"He's been looking for Tony."

"Why?"

"I don't know," I lied.

"What d'you mean looking for him?"

"I don't know. Maybe Tony owes him money. Anyway, it's not him."

"I don't like the sound of Carlin looking for my Tony!" He closed his eyes and slowly shook his head. "Jesus! Like I don't have enough to worry about!"

"Forget that for the moment."

"Easy for you to say. So. It's Doorrell!" He nodded slowly as if underlining a thought to himself. "Sounds about right!"

"Looks like it."

My head still hurt. I thought of something nice that might help it. I told Jack to ring me ASAP if the kidnappers made contact again. But I didn't think they would until we published the ad. I was at the door when a thought struck me. I turned and asked him how many people knew his house landline number.

"Only a few."

"That's what I thought."

I walked along the corridor, stood by Maxine's door and rang her.

"Hi, it's Eddie."

"Hello. I wondered if you'd ring."

"Where are you?"

"At work. And you ?"

"Outside your office."

There was silence for a few moments and then her door opened. She stood arms folded, leaning against the frame.

"Well! So you are." The body language said nice to see you. The eyes said it was more than just nice. I made a move to kiss her cheek. But she stepped backwards leaving my lips stranded and me feeling a little foolish.

"So how are you? Oh, I see someone's been in the wars. What happened?"

"A fight for life or death with three guys all at the same time."

"Yeah, right! You wouldn't be kidding me by any chance, would you!"

"I banged my head against a kitchen cupboard."

"Our hero! We had the police here yesterday. Did Jack tell you?"

"They question you?"

She nodded.

"What did you say?"

"What could I tell them? I'm just staff aren't I! What do I know about anything? Is that why you wanted to see me? Because of the law?"

"No. To ask you out to dinner."

"That's nice," and she smiled. It was such a lovely smile. It started at the lips as they drew back, then the eyes sparkled. "When did you have in mind?"

"When are you free?"

"I was planning on taking Friday off."

"Friday's good." She didn't want me to pick her up. So we arranged to meet at a bistro I know in Holland Park.

"Friday it is then." I hesitated for a moment, wondering whether to just say goodbye or try a peck on the cheek. Sort of a one-star kiss goodbye when she eased me towards her by my lapel and kissed me on the mouth. Nothing strong. But still, nice enough.

"Friday at 8 p.m. then," she said.

"I was thinking there for a moment you didn't do lips."

She brushed hers against my ear and in a low breath whispered,

"Well, Mister Sutton, you'd be wrong about that!"

Women! Go figure!

CHAPTER 20

I phoned the telephone number at the bottom of the back page of *Hot and Wet*, the magazine Arnie had given me. Told the switchboard I wanted to advertise in the mag and was put through to a guy with an Asian accent in sales. I told him my name was Harris from Personal Plastic Pleasure Ltd and we wanted to advertise with them. He started quoting prices for column inches.

"No. A full page. Maybe two. We plan on doing things big."

"Oh, right! Good."

"I've got a copy here of your May 2011 issue, page sixteen. The female pilot. We like the look of her. She could be the face for us. Our poster girl, if you will."

He said he'd have to find out who she was because all the women come through a model agency. The magazine didn't directly employ the girls. He asked for a number so he could come back to me with details and prices. I gave him the one of a telephone booth around the corner from my office and as I hung up thought – all the women in Doorrell's stable, and he still goes to an agency. Maybe!

Then I phoned Ricky and told him I wanted to see him and I'd be there in thirty minutes. While I was driving over, I wondered about him as a serious suspect for Davina's murder. Ex-boyfriend, angry at being dumped, maybe a dispute over drugs, money, maybe both. No forced entry. So she knew who she was letting in. It had all the right ingredients. By rights I should have dropped his name in Stafford's ear. But there would have been reverberations from that.

He was in jeans and a navy collarless shirt. The designer stubble was thicker. He showed me into his living room.

"What happened to your head?"

"Lenny Jordan. I saved him from a beating. Or worse, and this," I said, pointing to my temple, "was the thanks. Where is he? And don't give me the Trent House crap. He won't go back there. Because he knows Danny's looking for him."

He said he didn't know. But he wouldn't look at me as he said it.

"Where is he?" I demanded.

"I said I don't know!"

"You spoken to Davina Miller recently?"

"I'm not acquainted with any mediums."

"How d'you know?"

"I heard on the grapevine."

"Where were you when it happened?"

"Here, at home."

"How d'you know when it happened?"

"I, I, that is, someone must have mentioned when."

"If you say! When d'you last see her?"

"Ages ago!"

"If you say! I understand you two used to be an item."

"For a while." He shrugged and said, "Once upon a time!"

"You don't sound that upset about her being dead."

He shrugged again. I asked him what the shrug meant.

"Life, death, stuff happens."

So much for grief! So much for an explanation!

I followed him into the kitchen, which was large with

oak-panelled wall and floor units and black granite worktops. All a bit too heavy for my liking.

"Heard from Zoe?"

"Yes."

"So you know about …?"

"Yes."

"You people are in a whole lot of bother."

"Tell me about it!" and he sniffed. He pressed the percolator, opened a cupboard. "You want?"

"White, please."

He set out some mugs. The coffee clicked its way through the machine, sending a sweet warm aroma around the room.

"Why d'you set Tony up with Jordan?"

"Fuck you, Sutton! Fuck you!"

"If I was you, Ricky, I wouldn't swear at me again. You copy, Houston!"

He looked away, and poured the coffee.

"I've been a friend of Tony's for nearly two years. I didn't set him up. Jordan got paid five grand and was told he could keep whatever else he took. Plain and simple. If he'd have handed over the CD like he was supposed to instead of shaking Tony down, he wouldn't be in the shit he's in. So fuck him. He's got whatever's coming."

"Where is he, Ricky?"

"I told you; I don't know."

"That's right; you said."

I told him that Danny would probably take it out on Jordan by breaking both his legs. Because he couldn't hurt Tony or Houston as they were cash cows.

"For the moment," I added, just to try and put the shits up him.

"Too bad. That's show business. Milk?" He slid some over.

"Why did Tony want to go to Spain?"

"Who told you he did?"

"Davina's architect, Robin what's it."

"To keep her company, I suppose. How the fuck do I know! Ask Tony!"

"I would. Except someone's kidnapped him, remember! He ever let you drive his car?"

"Now and again. I just love that motor. Why d'you ask?"

"Just curious. Davina ever mention her father? Or what she might inherit?"

He sipped some coffee and told me she'd once mentioned that Ronnie had been living with some woman, a teacher or something, an ex-pat, in Du Casa for a couple of years and that they were in love.

"So maybe she went there to get her hands on stuff before the woman could."

"Such as?"

He looked at me over the rim of his cup.

"Who knows what Ronnie had stashed!"

"Do you?"

"Me? How would I know!"

"Let's hope you don't. Because you see the problem?"

"What problem's that?"

"Someone murdered Davina. And if my memory serves me correctly. The police will want to find out who did it. And motive is where they'll start. So if she came back from Spain with something that someone else wanted …You get my drift?

He went back into the living room and plonked himself in an armchair. I followed.

"There's something else, Ricky. Carlin finds out who killed her, it won't get to the Old Bailey because they'll be dead long before."

"Unless he did it."

"Why would he? He was banging her left right and face

down, and they were making pots of money. And then I had a second thought. With a 100 per cent of the business, he could always hire someone like a Davina, and if the someone was female and fucked in to the bargain. It was win-win for him.

"Shame someone didn't kill him!" Ricky said.

"Talking of Danny. Why did you see him the other night?"

"Not me!"

"Must have been your twin brother at Enfield dogs. If you can't think of a lie, the truth will do."

"You're a real smart arse, Sutton. D'you know that! One of these days …"

"I know. It's what everybody says. But today isn't going to be that day. So?"

He went to the window and stood there for a few moments just looking out.

"Well, you know most of the story. You might as well have the rest. He sent one of his regular gamblers, a tall thin redhead with a lot to say for herself, to the Freemont a few nights ago, who wanted a private word with Tony in the car park."

I could imagine. Right beside a car with some blokes in it to grab him.

"I told her he wasn't around and that she couldn't play until he was back. Jesus! I thought she was going to punch my lights out!"

"You're lucky she didn't. Her name's Collette Hammond and she doesn't do disappointment."

"I heard Carlin would be at Enfield. So I went there with a story that Maxine had sent Tony on a management course for a few days and that he shouldn't send any of his people to gamble until he was back."

"But he couldn't wait. So he grabbed Zoe."

His armchair was very comfortable and the coffee nice. But I was thinking of going, when he said,

"You got any ideas about Tony?"

"Some."

"Care to share?"

"No."

"Zoe said you'd mentioned a book. What's that about?"

"Nothing in particular."

"I'd be happy to help you look for it. If it'll help Tony. Is that what you think Davina went to Spain for? Or came back with? A book of Ronnie's?"

"You know what I think, Ricky? It's time for me to go." So I did.

I was walking back to my car when Arnie my snout phoned. I asked him how he was, and if he'd heard any gossip.

"Doorrell sent Blow Torch, one of his heavies, to Spain a few weeks ago."

"Blow Torch?"

"Fat Franky Farrel. Blow Torch is his nickname. Because that's what he uses on the soles of people's feet that upset Doorrell."

"Where in Spain?"

"Ronnie Miller Spain. They had a meet. He took him and his girlfriend to dinner talking business. Though I don't know about what. Arranged to go to the villa the next evening. But Ronnie kicked it during the afternoon. So Franky gets on the next plane home."

"Any chance he caused Ronnie's death?"

"No. Ronnie croaking was on the cards, weren't it!"

"How d'you mean?"

"He's mid-sixties. The girlfriend's forty and apparently a looker. That's nearly twenty-five years younger and tele's shit in Spain!"

"How d'you know all this?"

"Franky's missus has her hair done where a mate of mine's girlfriend works. She was going on about how pissed off she was. Because she thought she was going to get a long weekend in Du Casa. Instead gets three days of her Franky bitching about how he could have been in his local or at Spurs instead of wasting his time on Ronnie bleeding Miller! Any good?"

I wondered if Doorrell decided a death meant a will. And a will meant a beneficiary.

"Maybe," I said. "In the meantime I've got some work for you. I want you to follow a face named Ricky Houston for a couple of days." I gave him a description and an address. "How you fixed for transport?"

"I can get a moped."

"Who from?"

"Anyone that leaves one unlocked."

"Must be a bad line. I didn't hear what you said. If he goes to a casino called the Freemont, you can call it a day. Because he works there. I'll leave some dough for you at Steve's."

"We are talking cash?"

"Is there any other kind?"

"Cheers!"

CHAPTER 21

Thursday was the day for picking up Ronnie's book. It was bright with just a few clouds and a breeze. The trees surrounding Jack's house swayed a little and their branches cast moving shadows across the driveway. Jack looked dapper in a blue mohair suit, blue shirt, maroon tie and grey overcoat. He'd had a haircut since I'd last seen him. It looked nice and then he plonked a grey wool drop brim hat over it. Terry was in jeans, maroon zip-up and black boots, perfect for any aggro. I told Jack to get in the back of the Beema and at the first sign of any trouble to hit the deck.

"I'll be in the Jag," Terry said. "Never more than a couple of cars behind." He undid the zip-up. There was a sheathed knife hanging from his belt and a baseball bat on the car floor. Just lying there, brown wood against grey carpeting, the message clear. Any trouble from parties of the second part and they'd end up in hospital.

We exchanged mobile numbers and arranged to keep the phones on permanently. I told him I thought if there was going to be trouble, it would be on the way back, and he agreed.

Jack got in and I locked all the doors. We came through the Heath on to Hampstead Lane. The rush hour was over, the traffic light. I kept one eye on the road, the other on fellow motorists. I remembered the guys who had attacked Lenny Jordan and I started looking for white vans.

Jack was looking out of the window. I asked him if he was okay.

"The ad's out today. I wonder when they'll ring."

"They will. That's for sure." He looked pensive and I asked him if there was anything else on his mind.

"Ronnie. I've been thinking I should have gone to Spain for his funeral. You know, I knew him for nearly fifty years. I should have gone, regardless of how things ended between us."

I caught his face in the driver's mirror and he looked quite sad.

"We were both brought up in the same tenement building in Bethnal Green just after the war, went to the same secondary modern. That's how we became friends. No money. Just ambition to get out E2. And," he added, "ended up in the same line of business. Bet settling. Him for a national chain. Me for Sophie Freemont. That's where the name for the casino came from. Sweet old Sophie. She'd be tickled pink to know a West End casino had been named after her. One day Ronnie suggested we open our own betting shop. So we did. Then another, and another, and another."

"So how did you get into the casino business?"

He told me they were contacted by a firm of solicitors acting for a UK chain wanting to buy them out. They calculated that they could make so much money they almost decided to sell before they'd finished reading the letter. Then Ronnie reckoned if they'd made a shedload of dough from shops, they could make an even bigger killing with a casino or two.

"And we found one," Jack continued. "Our place in Brompton Road. The place was knackered. The business was knackered. The owners were knackered. But we knew what we could make of it. It started off as just a little spieler, cards, dice, bit of illegal horse betting. But we built it up into what it is today."

"Which is?"

"A licence to print money!" He looked out of the window at a few cars travelling in the opposite direction. "Maybe that was the problem. However much Ronnie made, it was never enough!"

We were halfway down Highgate Hill. Jack was checking his mobile again for messages. I'd been watching a blue Vauxhall a few cars back in my driver's mirror never less than three away. It wasn't the wooden cross hanging from the driver's mirror, although that's always a giveaway. It was the driver continually allowing cars out of side turnings to keep motors between us. I told Terry I thought we had company and I was just going to horse around. I took the next left, then a right and they came with me as did Terry but a long way back. I went down a one-way road that ended in a T-junction and indicated right. I made a big thing of twiddling the radio knobs while stationary as though looking for a station and as they passed to turn left and grabbed a surreptitious look. Not villains. Cops. I remembered one of the faces. A DC from Kingstone Road nick.

I came back onto Holloway Road knowing they'd be somewhere. Or there would be a second car clocking us. I asked Jack to slip his coat and hat off and pass them to me between the seats.

"You there, Terry?"

"Yeah!"

"They're cops. Wait until we get further down. Then pull up beside me." I told Jack I was going to make a big play of getting out of this car into Terry's who'd U-turn leaving him to drive to Finsbury Square. I asked Terry if he'd heard. He said, "Yes." I slipped on the hat and coat and another few hundred yards on said, "Now!" Terry pulled right out of the line and pulled up beside me. I got in the back of the Jag. He U-turned in front of an oncoming taxi that screeched to a stop. I looked out of the back window. Jack was already moving down a side street. There was a second car. A green Peugeot. The driver was good. Terry was better.

He gunned the engine and sped back up Highgate Hill.

"You're going to love this, Eddie. It's called audience participation. Right out the movies."

There was a zebra crossing ahead beside the Whittington Hospital with a couple walking their bicycles across it. He slowed. They got to the middle of it and Terry accelerated nearly over their toes, leaving the Peugeot to either stop or kill them. The woman fell over from fright dropping her bike. The man dropped his to help her. The Peugeot could do nothing but wait. Terry didn't have to. He turned left down Dartmouth Park Hill. I kept looking for the rest of the way. But he'd lost them.

We pulled into Finsbury Square off Moorgate. The sun was shining on the perfectly kept garden square. The grass looked like velvet. There were a few people stretched out taking latte al fresco with a fag. I checked faces. Nothing suspicious. The trees skirting the green still had leaves. The benches dotted around embellished the picture, making it all look like a little pocket of countryside right in the middle of busy screaming London. I looked for my Beema. It wasn't there. I was wondering if anything had happened to him when he drifted in. Cautiously, circled its three sides of white and cream-coloured seven-storey colonial-style buildings, then drove round again and parked beside us. I stood by the door looking around, smiling to myself feeling like one of those secret service types you see in the films guarding the President. All I needed was sunglasses and an earpiece.

"Any problems?" I asked, handing him his coat and hat.

"I knew I should have gone by tube. No!"

"Everything all right, guv?" Terry asked.

"Where d'you learn to drive like that? Kama-Kazi School of Motoring?"

"Not bad, was it! D'you see that cabby? I thought he was going to shit hisself. How long you gonna be?"

"No idea."

"Okay. You two go and do whatever. I'll be right here. Any aggro, Eddie, just holler down the phone." He looked competent, in command, perhaps even relishing an incident.

CHAPTER 22

Cornell, Buchanan, Halliday Solicitors were definitely what you expected for £750 an hour. Plus VAT. They occupied the whole of the ground floor of an entire office block. A steel- and armour-plated glass revolving door got you into the black marble lobby. Your name and who you were visiting got you past uniformed security and a couple of dozen paces got you into reception. There was huge walnut desk and a peach-coloured mirror behind it with their name engraved across it. And behind the desk a brunette in a green blouse with a big smile and even bigger tits. Funnily enough, it wasn't the smile I couldn't take my eyes off.

"Good morning, gentlemen. Can I help you?" My answer would have been 'You've no idea how!' But it wasn't me who spoke.

"Yes. I'm Jack Kreeger for Mr Allan Hampton."

"And you are?" she asked me.

"He's my carer," Jack cut in before I could speak.

She consulted a computer screen. Then tapped some keys on a phone.

"Mr Hampton. I have a Mister Jack Kreeger and a Mister Mike Carer to see you."

I started to say something. Jack put a hand on my arm.

"Don't. It's not worth the time it'll take!"

We walked down a thick-black-carpeted corridor and were met by a tall thin blond late twenty-something with a small pointed nose and nice smile. He wore round steel-framed glasses and a beautifully cut grey worsted suit, navy tie and a white shirt. His office reminded me a little of Jack's. It had a large wooden desk. A couple of green leather wing back armchairs, long casement windows.

We sat. He offered us coffee. Jack declined for both of us. He was asked for proof of identity and supplied all that he'd been advised to bring in the e-mail. Hampton had photocopies made and returned the originals.

"Unfortunate circumstances to meet under," he said. "I understand Mister Miller had a heart attack at his villa in Du Casa. His partner tried to help. Then rang for an ambulance. They took Mister Miller to a local hospital but he was dead on arrival." He made it sound so matter of fact. I suppose for him it was. "His will," he continued, "is quite clear how he wished to dispose of his estate. It was drafted by us some time ago. He required it drawn up in a manner to make incontestable."

Jack looked impassive, unconcerned who got what. But I was curious. So I asked.

"Normally, I wouldn't discuss bequests. But on the basis nowadays that you can find out these things with a click of the mouse and that if you pressed me you'd be entitled to read the will, I think common sense can be applied." He cleared his throat with a little cough and said, "His partner, a woman he had been living with for a while, got his villa and three million euros. His daughter, Davina Susanne Miller, got all his UK property. That's to say: six houses in North West London, and two blocks of investment flats in Ealing London W5."

That would have suited her very well, I thought, if it hadn't been for the fact that someone had bumped her off. And then it occurred to me what she'd meant in her phone call at her office, with GUESS WHAT I CAME BACK WITH. Not drugs. Not the book. "Several friends in Spain got twenty-five thousand euros each," he continued.

"Did his ex-wife or son get anything?"

He twiddled his glasses by one of its steel arms.

"No. As for you, Mister Kreeger, you were left a box containing a miscellaneous of things. Videos, jewellery, photos and a letter."

Jack and I looked at each other at the same time. We'd been expecting a book in the box. Not a lucky dip.

Hampton went to a safe and brought out a shoebox sized box wrapped in brown paper. The edges had been secured with duct tape and then tightly bound with white cord. Its edges sealing-waxed, then security-tagged. In other words it couldn't have been interfered with without it being obvious. He put it on his desk and we both just stared at it.

"In a moment I'm going to ask you to open the box and check its contents. Then invite you to sign two documents. The first that the inventory tallies with the items. The second receipt for possession. Clear?"

Jack nodded, but just kept staring at the box and I could only surmise that thirty- odd years of their hustling ran through his mind and was summarised in a box sitting on the desk of a man who wouldn't have even been semen when he and Ronnie started out. Jack bit his lip. Hampton asked him if he was okay.

"Perhaps I'll have that coffee after all!"

"Of course." Hampton went to a small trolley in the corner of the room upon which sat a percolator, crockery, spoons, sugar and a small jug.

Jack drank half in one go. It seemed to help.

"Are you okay to proceed, Mister Kreeger?"

Jack nodded.

Hampton slid the box across the desk together with a pair of scissors.

There were two DVDs, *Psycho* and *The Sound of Music*. A jewellery box, some photos and a letter. My first reaction was Ronnie had been taking the piss. Jack checked the inventory. But there were so few things; what could be missing?

"Do I owe you anything for this meeting?" he asked.

"No. Our fees come from Mister Miller's estate."

It was the first time I could ever remember a solicitor declining money. And I've known lots. Some with offices as comfortable and warm as his. Others so cold, the solicitors had their hands in their own pockets. He slid a ballpoint over and Jack signed both documents. He thanked Hampton, then shook hands with him. So did I and followed Jack out, carrying the box. I shot a look at the receptionist and decided I'd think of an excuse to come back like 'I was in here the other day. I didn't drop my mobile in Mister Hampton's office, did I? By the way what's your name …?'

Terry fell into step. We walked to the Beema with Jack between us. If there was going to be trouble, it would be from now on. He slid in the back. I locked the doors and took off. I watched him looking at the box.

"No book," I said. "Maybe Ronnie was just taking the Mike Carer!"

"I don't think so," he replied, checking his phone yet again.

I kept watching the road, expecting something at any moment. A lorry pulling out across us. A van braking in front with a couple of lunatics in face masks with baseball bats ready to have a go.

"You still there, Terry?"

"Yes."

"See anything?"

"Nothing."

The traffic was heavier than I'd expected. I hoped we weren't going to get stuck in a jam.

"You really expecting trouble?" Jack asked.

We were at Highbury Corner. Not that far from home. If anything was going to happen it would be soon.

A lorry began reversing its way out of a side road forcing us to slow.

"I see him," Terry said. "Anyone gets out, I'm out the Jag." But no one did. All there was, was a hand out of the passenger's window as a thank-you. A hundred yards along a motor cyclist whizzed past me too closely. And that was it! Twenty minutes later we were outside Jack's house with the gates locked behind us. I turned off the ignition and found I'd been holding my breath for the last few moments and blew a big sigh of relief at the windscreen.

CHAPTER 23

Lilly was in the hall dusting. Jack asked for a pot of coffee and a dozen sandwiches of whatever was easy to do. Terry disappeared. Jack checked his answerphone for messages. But there were none.

"Why don't you bastards ring!" he shouted at it. He laid the contents of the box on his desk, then pulled the letter from his pocket. It was in a small brown envelope with just his name scribbled across it. He slit it open and read it. A lump came up in his throat. He started to say something, but the words wouldn't come. He slid the letter to me and walked out of the room. I knew better to say anything or follow. I just sat and waited.

DEAR JACK,

IF YOU'RE READING THIS LETTER, IT'S BECAUSE, WELL, YOU KNOW WHY. WE HAD SOME GOOD TIMES. IN FACT, GREAT TIMES AND I COULDN'T HAVE LOVED YOU BETTER IF YOU WERE BLOOD. I HOPE THE PHOTOS BRING BACK SOME GOOD MEMORIES FOR YOU AS THEY DO FOR ME. GIVEN WHERE WE STARTED WE'VE BOTH PLAYED A BLINDER AS FAR AS LIFE IS CONCERNED. IT'S A SHAME THINGS WENT OFF A BIT AT THE END. I HOPE YOU CAN FORGIVE ME. THE VIDEOS MEAN A LOT TO ME. THEY WILL TO YOU. WATCH THEM ALL THE WAY THROUGH. AS FOR THE OTHER THING, YOU WERE THE BEST PERSON

TO GIVE IT TO. AND WHEN YOU FIND IT, YOU MUST DO THE BEST THING WITH IT. THAT'S TO SAY, WHAT'S RIGHT FOR YOU AND MAKES SENSE FOR YOU.

MAY BE ONE DAY WE'LL MEET AGAIN AND OPEN UP ANOTHER CASINO SOMEWHERE UP HERE WHERE AT LEAST THE PUNTERS ARE IN WITH A CHANCE.

TAKE CARE OF YOURSELF, AMIGO

Ronnie

Jack came back a few minutes later. His eyes were red. But he had control of himself. He picked up the *Psycho* DVD. It had the regular commercial cover with pictures of the film stars. He slipped it into the player and up popped the title and credits on his television. We were about ten minutes in to it when Janet Lee disappeared along with everything else. The screen went blank for a few seconds. And then different images appeared. A well-known MP who'd made his name campaigning against porn and promoting stronger anti-vice legislation lay stark naked on a bed propped up by some pillows while a black girl went down on him. She had long straight plaited hair which bounced gently against her vertebra as her head gently rocked back and forth. She moved aside. Her place taken by a big-breasted white girl, her face hidden by her hair, who finished him off. And his face with its square jaw and boyish grin convulsed in pleasure.

There was knock on the door. Jack turned the machine off. Lilly came in carrying a tray with a pot of coffee, crockery and a pile of sandwiches.

"Anything else, Mister Jack?"

"No. That's fine!" He turned it back on.

"Where d'you think this was shot?" I asked.

"In a flat he owned in Baker Street."

"How d'you know?"

"See the picture of the *Mona Lisa* above the fireplace beside the bed? He used to crack the same joke to everyone. 'It's not the original. It's just a print.'"

Next, up came a well-known Police Chief sitting in an indoor swimming pool of someone's house, with a blonde in his lap, dragging heavily on something that looked home-made. He handed her the fag. She took a deep, deep intake. So deep her tits fell out of her bikini top. Then he pulls the bottoms off and then his trunks off and they go at it. Then a picture of Ronnie in what looked like Jack's office handing over a manila envelope to a man. Then another picture of him in a park handing over an envelope to a uniformed police officer. And so it went on. Frame after compromising frame ending with apropos of nothing, pictures of headstones. Jim Benton 23rd February 1934–26th September 2009. 'Gone but Never Forgotten by his Loving Wife, Maude, Family and Friends.' And then there was the shot of another headstone. 'Elsie Thomas, born 15 January 1959, Gone to her Eternal Rest 28 March 2010. May She Rest in Peace.'

We stopped for some coffee and food. Surprisingly, watching all that porn had made me quite thirsty. *The Sound of Music* wasn't any better. But then I'm not a great lover of musicals. Maria von Trapp gave way to a Chinese girl face down on her knees getting it up the arse from a celebrated television interviewer. A few more shots of unknowns getting their rocks off. Then finally, a famous footballer lying starkers flat on the ground, arms akimbo, while a tall white girl with a cute little arse pissed over him. Twentieth Century Fox, this wasn't. But then this wasn't for your local multiplex.

I turned to Jack who was staring at me.

"So?" he said.

"It doesn't make sense!"

"That's what I'm thinking," he replied. "Okay, these people might be embarrassed if this stuff got out. The MP, the cop, might have to resign. It might even be blackmail currency. But kidnap, for this? Naaa! And what are those gravestones about?"

"Maybe we missed something." I said.

"Or could it be you just want to watch it all again?"

I smiled because he wasn't altogether wrong. I opened the jewel box, which was in burnished rosewood with a yellow abstract pattern inlaid in the lid. There was a gold Rolex inside. I handed both to him.

"This," he said, holding up the watch, "was a present from me to Ronnie to celebrate making our first million. Tight bastard never bought me anything." He looked at the TV screen again, then back at me. "So?"

I shrugged.

"Fucking Ronnie!" He picked up the box and hurled it across the room. It hit the corner of the bookcase, bounced off it and hit a chair and came to rest by the door. The impact must have triggered something inside the box because the bottom had slid open. There was a red leather notebook fitting so perfectly and so tightly in the base it couldn't move.

"This," I said, handing it to him, "I think you'll find is the star of the show." And it was, containing detail after detail. Names of serving officers, rank and station that Ronnie was bribing to ignore dealing at the Freemont. Officers on vice receiving backhanders from Leon. An address in Maida Vale where they could get their freebie servicing from a couple of Doorrell's girls. The user names and passwords of politicians, judges, doctors, lawyers subscribing to Leon's dating site, who were being blackmailed for their help when necessary. An address in St John's Wood used by two of Leon's girls to set men up for blackmail. The names of two separate planning officials who'd accepted presents, holidays, money to push through planning applications for a few of Ronnie's property developments. The amount of drugs and money going through the Freemont while Jack was abroad. The names and addresses of their best customers. And then when you thought it couldn't get worse – two names, Angela Elizabeth Barnes, and a Polish or Russian girl whose name I couldn't get my tongue around the pronunciation of, murdered by Leon. Buried by his brother. And that's what I suspected the two gravestones in the DVD were about. The girls' last resting place. Where, now free of Doorrell, they slept alone.

Jack slouched back in his chair waving the book at me. "Fucking Ronnie!" he said again. "This could get people killed! This is a list to die for!"

"It has already got people killed. Someone thought Davina had brought it back with her from Spain."

He finished his coffee and tuna and lettuce sandwich and said,

"You reckon?"

"I'm sure of it. She wanted you to sign that letter of authority, not because of the book, but in case there was any dough she could get her hands on."

He closed his eyes as if he'd momentarily gone off somewhere. And then he smiled as though an idea had transmuted itself into a plan. He opened them and the grin stayed fixed.

"What?" I asked.

"We go along with Doorrell's arrangement for the ransom, whatever that is. Then once I have Tony back safe and sound, I turn the tables on him."

"You're not going to do anything stupid, are you?"

"No. Nothing like that. I don't have to. Think about it, Eddie. He can't use Ronnie's stuff against me because the details in it incriminate him too badly. But I can use it against him because actually there's nothing in it about me thankfully. And anyway, I was abroad with a sick wife when all this happened wasn't I."

"So?"

"I'll type up a few facts and figures from the book and send it to him in an envelope with Freemont postal franking on it so he knows where it came from." He poured himself another cup and slid the sandwiches across to me." He may be Algerian," he continued, "but he'll understand the language I'm speaking."

"Which is?"

"Things have changed because I've now got the goods on him. Maybe I'll give him a few days for it to sink in, then contact him about buying the freehold of this place, just to make the point by just how much they've changed."

"But how are you going to hang onto the book and the DVDs if you have to surrender them for Tony?"

"By making copies."

I nodded slowly to myself. It was as simple as that! A shift of power. Not with a shooting, or a knifing, but with a photocopier!

"What about Danny?" I asked.

"I'll let him know. I can send him to prison any time I like."

"So you now take over from where Ronnie left off."

"I suppose so. With this," he said, waving the book in front of me, "I control everyone and everything. Just like a puppet master. They or their cronies put a foot inside my casino and I bring the curtain down on them!"

CHAPTER 24

Maxine turned up at the restaurant about five minutes after me. She was wearing a simple black cocktail dress. Well cut, close to the hips. The hem just above the knee. The neckline just a touch below modest, showing just a bit of cleavage, and gold drop earrings. The perfume was just a little sharp, but smelt classy and expensive. My guess was Dior's J'adore.

The lighting was mainly from the candlelit tables. The atmosphere was warm. Soft music played in the background. Slow melodic, pleasant, classical without being intrusive. We sat in a corner booth, secluded. She looked around and said,

"It's lovely, Eddie."

"I'm glad you like it."

She popped glasses on and looked at the menu. The waiter asked about drinks. I ordered two St Clements.

"You don't have to keep doing that, you know!"

"I want to. Besides, you're good for my liver."

"I'll take that as a compliment." She finished with the menu and dropped her specs into her bag and looked around again. "It's really nice. D'you come …?" She stopped dead.

"Do I come here often?"

She closed her eyes and flushed.

"Why did you ask me out?"

"Because I liked the look of you."

"Why d'you come?"

"You're the detective. Talking of which, any news?"

"Moving along."

"I've been trying to take as much work off Jack's shoulders as possible."

"I'm sure he appreciates it. He speaks well of you."

"We get along okay considering."

"Considering?"

"He took a chance on me. I took a chance on him."

She told me her name had cropped up several times when Jack had put out feelers for a general manager. That he'd interviewed her three times along with other candidates before offering her the position.

"He told me he'd back me all the way. He'd always be in my corner. I said I'd expect nothing less. And he has. I never forget loyalty. I never forget disloyalty for that matter!"

She looked wonderful. She smelt wonderful. But I could see the steel that had attracted Jack. She put her hand on mine and said,

"And now you're thinking what a hard, cold business bitch!"

"Not at all."

"What then? Or is that asking?"

"That you're the best friend a person could have. Genuine, honest, until they're disloyal and then they're dropped. Period. End of. No second chance." Her hand suddenly went cold.

"Jesus! What detective school did you go to?"

"Why?"

"That's pretty accurate. In fact, that's right on the money, Sutton. I can forgive anything but disloyalty."

"We're birds of a feather."

"Well, this bird is hungry."

"So?"

"The Dover sole, please."

"Your fish is my command!"

She smiled that megawatt smile. I just loved the way

she did. And I think she knew that I did. She looked across the table at me without speaking.

"What?" I asked.

"Just looking."

"Ongoing thawing?"

"Might be!"

She ate with gusto. Not quickly. But enjoying every mouthful as though there were a duty to do justice to the food. I asked about desserts. She asked what I was having. I said tiramisu, because it was my favourite. She said it sounded good. So that's what we had. We were nearly finished when I asked her if she'd like to come back to me for coffee.

"Where d'you live?"

"Regent's Park." Well! You can't be humble all the time can you?

"I'm nearer. Just up the road. Notting Hill."

She lived on the first floor of a huge period conversion. The common parts were carpeted in green. The walls papered in beautiful gold leaf. Her flat accessed by a wide circular Hollywood-style staircase. She showed me into the living room. A very female decorated space with pink drapes and pelmets across long casement windows. Soft magnolia-painted walls with a fifty-inch plasma screen in one of the two alcoves created by a striking white marble Adam fireplace and opposite a long rose-coloured settee, that beautifully complemented the drapes. Stafford had said that Residential Dreams' work was of a high standard. He was right. The flat was an absolute compliment to Davina's design talent. There was no centre light, just table lamps dotted around on side tables, and on them lots of photos. A middle-aged couple with their arms around each other. Maxine cheek-to-cheek with a slightly older woman. Another photo of her and the woman standing back-to-back, arms folded, smiling at the camera. And a group shot around a piano, all looking happy being in each other's company.

"Who are the photos of?" The couple were her parents, who lived in Hove. I asked if she saw them often.

"At least once a month and we speak at least once a week, minimum."

"And the woman?"

"That's Carole, my sister. She lives in Spain. She's been there years. I suppose you'd call her an ex-pat now."

"Whereabouts?"

"Du Casa."

"Du Casa?"

"Yes. It's not far from Gibraltar. Come into the kitchen. I'll fix us some coffee."

The kitchen was large and ultra-modern with white quarry-tiled flooring and built-in everything. I leaned against the grey granite worktop watching her.

"Milk, sugar?"

I slipped my arm around her waist and drew her to me and kissed her. She didn't resist. I ran my tongue very lightly down the side of her neck. She pressed closer. Maxine and the coffee began percolating at the same time.

Matters were continued on her settee. She certainly knew how to kiss, lips tongue teeth. There was a lot of touching and hand-roaming. But she wasn't prepared to take things into the bedroom.

"Something wrong?"

"It's been a while since I had a man in my life. Let's just see what happens." But nothing did. Well, nothing that I wanted to happen.

CHAPTER 25

I was in my office the following morning sorting out mail when Tom Stafford rang.

"What a coincidence, Chief Inspector. I was just about to ring you."

"Really! Well, I've saved you all that hard work of dialling. How's your memory?"

"I'm still trying to find out stuff for you."

"Shouldn't be too hard now."

"Why's that?"

"Gossip has it you're working for Jack Kreeger."

"Started yesterday. And you know you're right. He does have a son called Tony."

"So now you know two people by that name. D'you meet him?"

"He wasn't there."

"What you doing for Jack?"

"Advising on security, cameras, more bouncers, general stuff."

"Don't damage our friendship, Eddie. I want a word with Tony. Jack says he's in Bournemouth. But doesn't know where. So I want you to ask him to put him up."

I asked why me and he said because I could tell Jack how nasty and vindictive he, Stafford, could be when he tried.

"Street CCTV picked up a red Ferrari driving past her mews the day Davina was killed", he added. And we've got our boffins doing tests on her video entryphone. If he turns up on that, and with a bit of DNA, I think it's game, set and match. Oh! You can also tell him that all ports and airports have been alerted in case Kreeger junior decides to go on holiday."

I wanted to tell him why he couldn't interview Tony. Every bit of experience as a cop told me it was the thing to do. But I knew I couldn't.

"I'll ask," I said. "But why d'you think he'll listen to me?"

"Your charm. Your eloquence. And that his son is now prime suspect for the murder of Davina Miller."

"I'll ask."

"Does the word pronto mean anything to you?"

"That was the Lone Ranger's mate, wasn't it?"

"You should have been on the stage!"

"Any joy with the two names?"

"Zoe Fontaine. Two arrests in 2008 for prostitution. Fined the first time. Suspended the second. Nothing since."

"And Maxine Andrews?" Something inside me, for some reason, was hoping there wouldn't be anything.

"Too many with that name. Can't help you without a date of birth."

"Any joy regards Birmingham and Newcastle?"

"The police in Brum are checking on a few faces. As to Newcastle, we've got a line, if you'll excuse the terminology, on Carlin's supply of coke. I suppose I owe you one." And he hung up.

My phone rang again. It was Arnie with a progress report.

"It's what you gumshoes call it, isn't it?" I told him this was Camden Town not Hollywood. "The subject went to Wood Green this morning at 10 a.m."

"By subject, you mean Ricky Houston?"

"I do."

"Then speak English." I moved my letters over and put my feet up on my desk.

"He called at 78 Easter Avenue."

"And?"

"The subject, I mean, Ricky, tried the bell a couple of times. But no answer. Eddie?"

"Yes."

"You know, I'm getting a real taste for this working lark. Getting up in the mornings for a purpose. It's made me see another side of myself."

"They're good thoughts, Arnie."

"It struck me if I was earning regular from a job like this, I could rent somewhere instead of dossing or squatting. I could even end up on an electoral register one day! You don't need a full-time assistant, do you?"

"Not right now. But if things change, I'll let you know."

"I'll keep following Houston and find out about the house. Over and out!"

CHAPTER 26

I was about two hundred yards from Steve's, when a guy about seven foot with a barrel chest and a face like an ad for Hallowe'en stepped in front of me.

"My boss would like a word."

I looked over his shoulder at a stretch limo at the kerb. It was big and black and shiny like the guy.

"My mum told me never to speak to strangers."

"Well, once you've met him you won't be strangers any more, will you. Besides, if I wanted to hurt you, you'd already be hurt." And he pointed to a guy much smaller, only six foot something, leaning against a wall behind me. "Now please!" He opened the door and I slid in. The interior had two long white leather seats opposite each other. Hi-fi speakers in each corner and a pull-out bar, pulled out.

He was in his late thirties, dark-skinned, but not black. Short cropped hair brushed off his face, greying at the temples. Dark almond-shaped eyes, almost female, and a broad smooth nose set between narrow cheekbones. Moustache, goatee beard, both flecked with grey. Leon Doorrell. He wore a light grey tonic mohair suit, white shirt, charcoal-grey tie. The shoes were black leather. They looked expensive. So did he, and aggravation.

"My name's Leon Doorrell. I thought we'd have a word."

I sat down and looked at him thinking how you'd get out of there if he didn't want you to. The answer was simple. You couldn't.

"Coincidence, you driving by as I happened along."

"Nothing in my world happens by accident, Mister Sutton. I was told the snooker club was a haunt of yours. I've had someone following you from your office. They phoned to tell me where you were headed. I understand you're still working for Jack?"

"I haven't actually seen him since the approach from your personnel department."

"Oh, yes. Victor."

Something told me he wasn't here for violence. Not today. Otherwise Victor would be instead.

"A change of plan. I'd like you to continue at the Freemont."

"Because?"

"You'd be able to help me."

"Help you?"

"I'm not going to ask what you're doing for Jack. Because I probably wouldn't get the truth. But you obviously have his ear at the moment."

"So?"

"Owning the Freemont fits very well with my business plans. But he won't sell."

"Sounds like that's that, then!"

"I'm not used to people saying 'no' to me." His voice was deep, almost bass and monotone. But it carried a menace from the vocal cords to the tip of his tongue.

"No disrespect, Mister Doorrell, but I don't see how I can help."

"By being my eyes and ears."

"I got the impression from Victor you already had eyes in the Freemont." Because that's how Victor had known to wait for me. I wondered whose they might be. Zoe was first to mind. And then, for some reason, Maxine. Though realistically it could have been anyone, from someone on reception to one of the bouncers.

"I need to know what skeletons he has in his cupboard as a means of persuading him to sell."

"Blackmail!"

"Drink?"

"No, thanks."

He poured himself something.

"I call it giving him reasons to sell." He raised the glass and knocked back half. Then started to tell me how he'd come to England with his mother and brother from Algeria as immigrants. That his first job was at fifteen in a menswear shop.

"A man comes in for a blue striped shirt, Mister Sutton. We don't have any. So I sell him a white one. What colour did he want?"

"Blue."

"White. Because that's what I persuaded him he really wanted. That's what I still do, Mister Sutton, persuade people to see things my way."

I didn't care for the way he kept saying Mister Sutton. He made it sound like the name of an illness.

"You'll let me know what you hear that can help me and you'll find me not ungenerous. Especially for the right information." He pulled a Manila envelope from a side pouch in the door and dropped it in my lap. "Fifteen thousand. And another fifteen for the right story."

I was wondering how to say 'no'. The how was important, because I didn't know if he had a temper or if he carried a weapon. After all, I'm sitting in a limo with tinted windows. The doors probably locked. And if something happened to me, pedestrians six feet away wouldn't know.

"That's very generous of you, Mister Doorrell, but let me leave the money with you for the moment. If I can help I know you won't welch on your word. That way it gives me time without being under pressure to produce something because of the fifteen." It sounded plausible. It was the best I could do on the spur of the moment.

He finished his drink, stroked his goatee as his eyes tried to read the truth in mine, and gave me the benefit of the doubt.

"Don't keep me waiting too long. I don't do waiting, Mister Sutton!" He knocked on the glass partition and tall, dark and cyanide, who was now behind the wheel, released the door locks.

I got out and Doorrell lowered the window and handed me a card.

"I never forget people that help me, Mister Sutton. Or those that don't." And the motor glided away with the six-foot- six job following in an XJS. I stood on the pavement shaking, sorry I hadn't taken up his offer of a drink. I took some deep breaths to try and calm myself but I still shook. But a few more helped the shakes pass and when they had, I had two thoughts. He didn't have Tony either. And – so what now?

I watched his hundred-grand motor disappear into the traffic and told myself I must have missed something between Danny and Doorrell. I went through the scenario and cast of characters again, looking for what I wasn't seeing. I was still busy at it when my phone trilled.

"Is this Eddie Sutton?"

"Who wants to know?"

It was Lenny Jordan the petty thief who'd lifted Carlin's CD. I looked at my phone as though it could confirm reality.

"You got some front ringing me, Jordan!" My fingers went instinctively to my temple. The swelling had subsided. But not enough to be completely pain-free. "What's the call for? Hoping for the chance to cave in the other side of my head?"

"Sorry about that!"

"Sure! You sound heartbroken."

"I thought I might be able to do us both a bit of a favour like, Sutton."

"How d'you get my number?"

"You've got a website, haven't you? 'Eddie Sutton. Private detective. Discreet, experienced, affordable'"

I had a mental image of the courtyard at his flat and the moment I'd turned around to look for him and was hit with the brick.

"So. What's this favour?"

"I hear you're looking for Tony Kreeger. I know who's got him and where he's being held."

"Where?"

"It'll cost you ten grand."

"Really. You're not exactly Mister Dependable, are you, Jordan!"

"This is legit."

"Of course!"

"On the level."

"Five."

"Ten!"

"Five. And I'm being a fool to myself. Because if I had the time and more sense, I'd find out where you are and come round and break your legs to get the information."

"Okay, five! I'm sorry about the other day, Sutton. I just got so scared after those guys tried to grab me."

"Cue the violins! So, where and when?"

"Tonight. 8 p.m. Luigi's Pasta. Newnham Street, back of Turnpike Lane tube. Come alone."

"You too, Jordan."

I wondered what the scam was. Because you could no more trust Lenny Jordan than you could trust a Bill Cosby drink. But it was the sort of circumstance you had to go along with, even though you knew it was going to end in a big no-no. And then there was the CD. No five grand until I got that as well.

I walked the few hundred yards to Steve's snooker hall. Had a pint and spent the rest of the afternoon playing and wondering yet again about Doorrell. I was sure he had Tony. But the episode in the car changed that. Then my thoughts turned to Lenny Jordan and tonight.

I went home to get my stuff together. Five thousand in cash from the money Jack had given me. The snub-nosed gun I kept wrapped in foil in my fridge and the shells in a large brown plastic bottle camouflaged by fifty or so paracetamol.

I don't like carrying a gun. Because if you do, you're likely to end up using it. Armed police officers aim for the chest because that's the largest single area on a human. That's why a lot of their victims die. But a bullet in the leg or legs is pretty persuasive. Trust me! When the bone splinters and the blood gushes and the pain starts it tends to concentrate the person's mind about carrying on. All that, and the chances are they don't die. Nevertheless, discharging a firearm is not good and is to be discouraged, and like I say, I'm not keen. But there are occasions …

The pizza restaurant was at the end of a parade of secondary units at the corner of a narrow turning leading to an open council car park free after 6.30 p.m. The buildings along the street were boarded-up shops, and two small light industrial units with metal roller shutter fronts. The only light, orange haze from two street lamps and a third in the car park. I wondered how safe my Beema would be in there. But the main road was full so there was no choice.

The diner was warm, bright and looked clean. There were no table or chairs, just booths along the walls and down the centre of the room. Dean Martin played in the background giving it his full Italian repertoire. It all reminded me of the old-fashioned Italian restaurants in American gangster movies. Pleasant, homely, everyone enjoying themselves until two guys in fedoras and double-breasted suits with machine guns walk in.

The place was half full but there was no Lenny. I waited ten minutes nursing a beer. Then ordered fettuccine in pesto. Dean Martin started another number with an accordion and violin support and just audibly accompanied by two waitresses waiting for the bell from the kitchen. I finished the meal. My watch read 8.45 p.m. I checked my mobile for messages. Two. Neither from him. By 9 it was clear he wasn't coming. I supposed I shouldn't have expected anything better. Perhaps it was about getting me out of the way while someone searched my flat and office. Well, if that was the plan, they'd be unlucky, because both were as secure as a nun's knickers.

I walked up the narrow road back to my car when I heard a motor behind me, headlights obviously full on, because part of the buildings either side were suddenly bleached with light. I turned to find it was heading straight for me. The little fucker's coming for me, a voice in my head screamed. I stepped onto the pavement. It mounted it, two wheels on, two wheels in the road.

I darted across the street and charged one of the boarded-up doors with my shoulder with fourteen stone behind it. But it didn't even creak, never mind give. My mouth dried. My scalp tightened as the car got closer. The threat of flesh and bone, my flesh and bone, fused with rubber and steel sent even more adrenalin into my veins. The sweat from the running and the fear ran down my face. I swiped at my eyes and brow with my sleeve. Sweat ran down my back, soaking my shirt. There was reflux from the pasta and beer and the awful taste of stomach acid filled my mouth. I spat but couldn't get rid of it. I charged another door in total panic. But that held too. I tried the handle of a third. No luck. The road was full of shit properties you wouldn't look twice at, yet all were secured like this was Threadneedle Street!

I zigzagged between road and pavement. The car was now just feet away. I flattened myself against a shop doorway in desperation and because of no other option. There was a loud crunch as it took a large piece of the wooden frame away. Then a clang from the bumper coming off the kerb, then an even louder sound from the clutch grating. The engine stalled. There were two attempts to restart it that failed. The third succeeded. The wheels whirred trying to grip the asphalt, then engaged, reversing the car to give it space to come at me again. In the meantime I'd managed to run on a further few yards. Tried another door that was locked. I got to a pavement electric junction box and crouched behind it. Took some deep breaths, then a few more, rested my arms on top of it with both hands around the butt of the snub-nose. I fired once at the passenger side while trying to see who was driving, but the Triplex windscreen shattered in a cobweb of glass. The refraction of orange street light making abstract patterns across the undamaged parts. The car swerved left. The hub caps smashed against the kerb. I wondered if I'd killed the driver. But no, because the car began reversing right back down the road, its headlights sweeping the buildings. I fired again, this time into brickwork just to really put the shits up him or her. The car got to the mouth of the turning, swung wildly out into the main road and was gone.

I sat on the pavement, my back supported by the junction box, closed my eyes and held my head in my hands. I would like to have stayed like that for a good long while to gather myself. But knew I had to move because if anyone had reported 'what sounded like gun shots' to the cops, they'd be down here in minutes.

I got to my car, took a quick swig of Scotch from a bottle in the glove compartment and headed home. "Should have got the number plate," I told myself. "Like you had time," the sensible side of me replied. But the sensible side couldn't dissuade me from what I'd do to Lenny Jordan when I got my hands on him. And then I had another thought. Whoever had Tony had made their first mistake. Because Jordan was connected to the kidnapping. And when I found him I'd make him talk.

CHAPTER 27

Maxine and I had a second date. To the cinema, a few days after our meal, on a free afternoon of hers. The film was a spoof detective. We yawned at the same time. She apologised. Then so did I. We decided to skip the last ninety minutes and went back to hers. I didn't know what to expect because she'd been reluctant to let things go too far after the meal. She said she had to leave around 7 p.m. for work. So I supposed I was a fill-in until then. She made coffee. We sat on the settee. I asked how she'd got into the casino business. She'd been a bored clerk in a building society. Saw an ad for trainee croupiers in the local paper and absolutely loved it from day one. Three years in, she joined a cruise liner and met her future husband, also a croupier.

"Peter Elliot Marshal," she said. "I thought we were happy. But obviously not."

I asked what had happened. Then apologised for being nosy.

"It's okay. I'm past it. He ran off with another croupier a week after our fifth wedding anniversary that he'd spent telling me how much he loved me."

"Jesus!"

"I took it very badly. I thought it must be all my fault. I started drinking. Until …"

"You found out drink's not the answer."

"Sounds like you've been there."

"Once."

"What I discovered is that the answers to your

problems, to most problems, lie in the view you have of yourself. Change that and you're on the road to repair. At least, I was." She topped up my cup from a pot and said, "I have a confession to make. I ran you through Ubex."

"Ubex?"

"It's a vetting agency we use before hiring staff."

"So now you know about my years in the Foreign Legion and five ex-wives."

"I must have missed that bit."

I couldn't make up my mind whether I was annoyed or not.

"Interesting reading?"

"Oh, yeah!"

"Do you do that with all the chaps that take you to dinner?"

"Depends."

"On what?"

"The chap!"

"So?"

"Forty-one. Single. Joined the police at seventeen as a cadet. Rose to Detective Constable. Asked to resign five years ago for conduct incompatible with Metropolitan Police standards."

"Is that what it said?"

"What does that mean? Did you take a bribe or something?"

"I chinned a drug dealer. Actually, that's not true. I put him in hospital for three days."

"Any particular reason? Or is this the Met's new interviewing technique?"

"He was responsible for the death of a nineteen-year-old Danish au pair, who he got hooked on dope then pimped."

"Sounds like he had it coming."

"He did. All dealers do in my opinion. But you're still

not allowed to do it." I wondered how finding out about a bit of violence might play. But she didn't seem put out.

"And a commendation once from the Commissioner of Police no less," she continued, "for saving a baby's life. Something about a coked-up mother throwing her baby on a railway line. Apparently it said all the waiting passengers froze because of an incoming train. Except you, who jumped on the line, threw the baby to a porter on the platform and just managed to jump clear of the train. That takes some balls."

I didn't say anything. Because what can you say!

"Is it true?"

"Anyone would have done it."

"I don't know anyone who would have. And I know a lot of people."

"It's all in a day's work."

She sat there looking at me. Silent. Admiration? Respect? I couldn't read it.

"It must have been tough parting from an organisation like the police. Must be like suddenly losing your family, I would have thought."

No one had understood that before. Or the uncertainty or dread about the future it creates. She asked about my real family. But there wasn't a lot to tell. Parents dead. Younger brother with a marriage in trouble because their daughter had met someone like Joey Farmer, the guy I'd beaten up. She kept looking at me. I asked what she was thinking.

"About you jumping on a railway line to save a baby's life."

"Oh, that! This Ubex thing. Is there anything else I should know about myself?"

"Just this!" She leaned over and kissed me. A real creamy, lipsticky smackeroo. "I think that about covers everything."

I drew her to me and kissed her. And she kissed back as if she really meant to kiss. As if those lips had really found something they wanted to engage with. She slipped off her shoes and sat astride me.

"You know, you're okay!"

"Have I just been paid a compliment?"

"You're the detective!"

She wore a very thin grey shirt which I began unbuttoning.

"What you doing?" she asked.

"You must be so hot in this!"

"You know, you're right, I am. You must be hot too."

"Boiling!"

"Then we'd best have this shirt of yours off, don't you think!"

It was a bit like the domino theory. A piece of her clothing came off precipitating a piece of mine. Then hers, then mine. The last dominos, my boxers, her panties metaphorically and literally fell in her bedroom.

She lay on her stomach. I kissed the nape of her neck then ran my fingers down her long powdered body, my nails lightly engaging with the nerve ends in her skin. She turned over and I kissed her breasts, large firm, almost buxom. I licked her nipples, thick, stiff, inviting. I ran my hands down her stomach and spread her thighs. After my fingers had been inside her I slipped a wet tongue there and began licking slowly, gently, just sliding back and forth , back and forth, and then just ever so slightly stronger. She wrapped her arms around her head as her breathing became heavier and heavier and then she went into orbit moaning, "Dear Christ in heaven!" Then "Don't stop, please don't stop!" Then later "Take me, Eddie, take me!" And I did. She grabbed my hair in her fists and pulled me close, closed her eyes and biting her bottom lip was off somewhere again. First it was me on top of her. Thrusting demanding, taking. Then her on top of me. Shaking, shrieking, wriggling, licking, biting, almost out of control. Each of us happy to let the other have their take. Locked in lust. Lost in pleasure. Thrashing, sweating, just absolutely rampant! And then when I thought it couldn't get much better we came together, her with an orgasm I thought was going to blow her circuits!

We lay exhausted in the near dark. The room lit by a street light through not quite closed curtains. She held a hand to her forehead and said,

"Jesus! You've no idea what you just did to me!"

"Did to you good? Or did to you bad?"

She rolled on top of me and smiled.

"You, Mister Eddie Sutton, are just fishing for a compliment, aren't you?" She closed her eyes and let out a long low sigh as if the pleasure hadn't finished flooding through her. "And why not?" she finally breathed.

I kissed her and had an urge to tell her that this had been more than just another scalp. This had been different. But I knew it would sound corny. She ran her hands through my hair, then traced a finger around my mouth.

"Look at that tongue! Oh boy, what a naughty, naughty tongue. Hmmm! The less said about it the better, I think." I started to speak. She put a finger across my mouth. "I don't think you should waste those lips on words."

So I kissed her with a kiss that had it been any stronger would have bonded us together.

"And how do I go to work after this?" she said. "I'll walk in with a huge grin on my face and everyone will know what I did this afternoon."

"Do you have to go?"

"I do. I'd rather not, believe me," she said, propping herself on her elbows. "I'd just like to stay here and roll around naked with you all night, Mister Private Detective!"

And the thought of us at it all night set the juices flowing and the hydraulics back into operation. "But I have to." She put a hand on my arm and said, "Don't be upset."

"It's okay!"

"Is it? When will I see you again? Will I?" she said. "I guess I'll just have to wait on that, won't I?"

"Well, now. Let me think. Julia Roberts, Monday. Kate Moss, Wednesday …"

"Ha, ha! Are you seeing anyone at the moment?" She pulled a face and said, "None of my business. I shouldn't have asked."

"I am actually."

"Should have guessed. Well, at least you're honest."

"She's very nice."

"Really? Like I want to know!"

"She lives in Notting Hill. She's the general manger of a casino."

"Very funny. Aren't you the comedian!"

"I'm not, seeing anyone, that is."

"Good." She shrugged and said, "What I mean is. That's okay. Because I'm not seeing anyone at the moment as it happens. That's what I meant by good."

"Why don't you come over to me one evening and I'll make you a meal."

"Cooks as well!" she exclaimed at the ceiling.

"Nothing very grandiose. Just the best pasta you'll ever taste!"

"Now, how's a girl supposed to refuse an offer like that!"

CHAPTER 28

So she went to work, and I went to Steve's. I sat at the bar and all I could think about was her. Us.

"I said, what'll it be. Hello, anyone home?"

"Sorry, Steve. I was miles away. Scotch, please." I handed him an envelope. "This is for Arnie."

"Lolly?"

"Yup!"

"How's he working out?"

"He's okay. Fancies himself as a private eye."

"Don't they all. The next thing you know he'll be asking for a job."

"He has." Steve stuck the envelope in his trousers. "You don't need anyone, do you?"

"I got little Harry helping behind the bar here, and his missus making sandwiches and pies. That's all I need. Why don't you ask someone at that Freemont gaff?"

"Good idea. And I know just who." And she popped into my mind again. But not for long, because a pal of mine, Carl Harris, who was tall with a beer gut, put his hand on my left shoulder and as I turned around to see who it was, drank half my Scotch from the right.

"Fancy a game, Eddie boy?"

"Why not. Always a pleasure taking your money."

"Yeah, yeah! I could beat you with an erection never mind a snooker cue."

"How far's half an inch going to get you?"

"Steve!" he shouted. "I have a man here pleading with me to take his money. What table do you have free for me to perform the annihilation on?"

So I spent the evening playing. I wasn't on my game. Because she was on my mind to the point that I phoned her.

"Hello. I was told this was the number of the sexiest woman in Knightsbridge."

"And you'd be?"

"The name's Sutton."

"Sutton, Sutton. The name rings a bell. Oh, yes! Well, this is a pleasant surprise."

"I'm full of them."

"I just bet you are!"

"Thought I'd ring see if you got to work okay."

"I swear everyone in this place knows what I was doing this afternoon, Eddie."

"Paranoia."

"Flushed cheeks make-up won't hide. Where are you? Anywhere nice?"

"In a friend's snooker club in Kilburn."

"Have you been thinking about me?"

"You may have crossed my mind."

"I've been thinking about you. I'm looking forward to the meal, Eddie." She paused. I got the impression she was thinking about what she was about to say. "Was that the truth about not seeing anyone at the moment?"

"Scout's honour! Why? Would you be upset if I was?"

"Maybe. Maybe not. It's a free country."

"I'm not."

"Good. How does Sunday sound for cooking pasta?"

"Fine."

"Hang on a moment." I could hear her saying 'come in' and inviting someone to have a seat. "Gotta go, Eddie. Maybe we can speak tomorrow." She said bye and blew a kiss, and I found myself absentmindedly trapping it on my lips with my finger.

CHAPTER 29

I was in my office, feet up on my desk, drinking coffee and trying to make sense of everything. Tony had now been held for five days. We'd had a phone call for the ransom. We'd let them know we now had the book. But we'd heard nothing since and neither of the prime suspects was the kidnapper and yet someone had tried to kill me. This wasn't like any snatch I'd heard of. It went through my mind Tony might be dead. But then, why kill him? I took a sip and was considering the alternatives to Danny and Doorrell when the phone went. I hoped it was Maxine. I was looking forward to speaking to her. It was Arnie.

"How you doing?"

"Good. Thought I'd update you."

"You're learning the jargon. I left an envelope for you with Steve. May even be able to get you a job through a friend of mine."

"That's real good of you, Eddie. You know, no one ever put themselves out for me before unless there was an angle in it for them."

"No promises, Arnie. All I can do is ask."

He kept thanking me. Then said he was near the house again in Wood Green and that it was owned by a Miss Pauline Jordan.

"Jordan! How d'you know?"

"Gave the postman a fiver! Told him I was a private detective on a case. I'm across the road. There's been something going on inside," he continued.

Miss Pauline Jordan, I repeated to myself. Had to be

Lenny's sister. Because if she was married, there'd be a different surname. And if she was married but still using her maiden surname, it still made her his sister, and where better to hole up.

"There's a white van parked outside with Acme Builders on it," Arnie continued. "And there's a couple of blokes now just hurrying out."

I took my feet off my desk and sat up straight.

"What do they look like?"

"Like a right pair of geezers, if you know what I mean."

"Okay, Arnie, split! You're in danger. Go and don't go back."

"It's okay. Maybe I'll just hang around. See what I can see."

"Arnie, listen to me. Clear off!"

"I'm into this, Eddie, I'll be all right."

"No, you won't. Go to Steve's. He's got a nice big envelope with lots of mazoola in it. Go get it." Arnie's safety wasn't the only reason for wanting to get rid of him from there. The other was that I didn't want any witnesses to my 'conversation' with Lenny!

I grabbed my jacket and made it to Wood Green in twenty. Easter Avenue was a turning behind a shopping mall in the high road. A street of Victorian two-storey terrace houses with square bay windows and four-foot brick walls dividing them from the pavements. Same after same either side of the street. The only differentiation the colour of the front doors. There was a parked moped opposite number 78. But no Arnie. I knocked. No answer. Twice. Nothing. I cupped my hands against the window glare. Lenny Jordan lay on the floor, propped against a wall. His hands up as if someone was holding a gun on him. But there was no one else in the room. I knocked. No reply so I kicked the front door open. I waited a moment. Still nothing.

Everything looked normal except for an upturned armchair. Oh, and Lenny, who lay on the carpet with hands either side of his head secured to the wall with masonry nails through the palms. His blood had spattered the wall, making red irregular shapes on the magnolia emulsion. Gobs of it ran down his hands, his wrists, and disappeared down his arm leaving a thin red stripe on his shirtsleeve. His nose had a gash across it. His lips were blooded and swollen. He'd also taken a kicking in the chest, because there were black boot or shoe prints on his shirt front. My first thought was what a shame someone had got there before me.

I checked for a pulse. He was still alive. He opened his eyes.

"Why d'you set me up, Lenny? And where's the CD?"

He fell forwards. But couldn't get far.

"Don't know what talking about," he burbled.

"You want help with these nails? Or d'you want to wait until they fall out the wall of their own accord? Why d'you set me up? Was it Danny?"

"Told them Ricky's got it."

"The CD? Where!" I yelled. "Tell me. Or I'll leave you here for Carlin's men. If you're still alive when they come back."

He must have considered me the better option. Because he motioned with his head towards a CD rack beside the hi-fi opposite.

"George Michael!"

"Who ordered you to set me up?"

He passed out.

I tried gently shaking him, then slapping his face. Not lightly like they do on the films. But a good, hard palm job. But he was completely out of it. So I put on a pair of white latex gloves that I always carry with me and started going through the CDs. *Spinning the Wheel*, *Faith*, *Listen Without Prejudice*, on and on. One after another. I hadn't realised George had made so many albums. I shot the occasional look over at Jordan, his head slumped, still unconscious, his breathing shallow. The wounds had started bleeding again. It was all I could do to stop myself from giving him a good hard kick in the chest and maybe finish him off. At last, *Patience*, how apt, had Carlin's CD pinned underneath it. I slipped it into my pocket and using Jordan's landline, dialled 999.

"Ambulance." I told them there was a guy at 78 Easter Avenue, who'd had his hands nailed to a wall. The despatcher asked if this was a joke. I said it wasn't. And that his name wasn't Jesus either. "He's lost a lot of blood. He's in shock and keeps slipping in and out of consciousness. Right now he's unconscious." I repeated the address, hung up and left.

CHAPTER 30

I was about to play the CD on my office player when the phone rang.

"Is that the sexy detective agency where clients are guaranteed complete satisfaction?"

"I try my best."

"Your best gets full marks, Sherlock."

"So, Ms Andrews, what can I do for you?"

She laughed a very dirty laugh and said,

"Want a list? Thought I'd ring see how you were."

"I'm good. Where are you?"

"In bed."

"What d'you have on?"

"Just the radio!"

I had a mental image of her stark naked underneath the sheets. The boobs, that face, framed by ash-blond hair, lying against a pillow. Cosy, warm and ripe.

"Maybe I should come over, make sure you're tucked in tightly."

"'Fraid not. My sister Carole's over from Spain for thirty-six hours. So we're spending the day together. Lunch, retail therapy, all good girly stuff!"

"Thirty-six hours. Hardly worth coming."

"She's here to sign some papers regarding a property. Has a lawyer and a few people to see. Then we've got some business to take care of with someone in South London. Then she's going on to Hove to stay with Mummy and Daddy overnight. Then flying home."

"Where's home, remind me?"

"Du Casa. So you'll just have to restrain yourself until Sunday. But I'm sure I'll think of something to make it up to you, because I'm really looking forward to seeing you."

"I'm looking forward to seeing you." And I had to admit to myself that I was.

"Here's a kiss on account. The rest to be delivered in person." Then she blew me another.

"That was two."

"So it was. I wonder what that means? Sunday then!" I replaced the receiver. But I couldn't get that word Du Casa out of my head. I'm not a great believer in coincidences although they happen. On the other hand, there were bound to be more than one ex-pat living there. So why not? Or was I just trying to tell myself she couldn't be involved?

I slipped the CD into the player.

"The dough or the coke, Tony. Simple as that!" Carlin was saying.

"I don't have either as you well know."

It felt funny hearing Tony's voice at last. So far all he'd been was a photo and the subject of other people's experiences. He had an ordinary middle-class London tone with good pronunciation. There was the sound of a chair falling over. I imagined Danny picking Tony up by his shirt front or jacket lapel.

"Well, you best find one or other. Got it, sonny? My coke or four hundred grand."

"Four hundred?"

"Interest!"

"I just don't have it."

"By the end of the week. Or I'll introduce you to a friend of mine. She hurts people, Tony. She'll hurt you. She'll hurt you in ways you didn't think possible. You'll tell her things you didn't even think you knew! Just to get her to stop the pain. Good-looking boy like you, late twenties. She'll make a meal of you."

"You won't touch me."

"Why? Because of Daddy? Maybe I'll hand him over to her as well. He's overdue in my opinion." There was a scuffle, and what sounded like another chair going over. Someone gasping, probably Tony. "Or maybe on second thoughts I'll just tell Jack what his entrepreneurial son has been up to and collect from him. Yes. I think that's what I'll do."

"He'll tell you to go fuck yourself."

"You reckon? We'll see, shall we?"

"No, don't. Please don't."

"Friday, or else. Now clear out."

"I have an investment flat in Hammersmith. I'll sign it over to you." There was a pause and Danny asked how much it was worth. "Two hundred and fifty thou."

"It still leaves you a hundred and fifty short."

"Please, Danny, I don't have anything else. I can't let my old man know" and he started crying.

"Friday. Now scram! Wait! I've just thought of something. Maybe there is a way."

"How?"

"Yeah! Now I come to think of it." He paused as though he was thinking things through. Though he knew the next few lines full well. "You let a few of my people come down to the Freemont and win at the tables, five, six grand a time, nothing heavy. Until we get to, say, half a mil. Debt cleared."

"Half a mil!"

"Interest!"

"I don't know. If my father found out …"

"What's to go wrong? They'll play at tables where you're the pit boss. You must have mates that will help."

"I don't know."

"Suit yourself. Friday it is!"

"Wait!" There was a long silence. Then Tony said he'd

do it.

"When?"

"It'll take a week or so to set up."

"That's okay. No sweat. Now that we understand each other." Danny's voice was now warm and friendly, like an SS officer assuring an inmate 'it was just a little old shower room'. "One other thing," he continued. "You'll need to turn a blind eye to a couple of my people approaching your richer clients about their requirements."

"Dealing!"

"It'll be discreet. No need to wave our business under everybody's noses." There was a fawning little laugh and he added, "What d'you know! I just made a funny!" And someone laughed in the background. "Dave here'll give you a number to ring for when you're ready." There were blips as Tony keyed it in. "Good. It'll all work out, trust me." And a door opened. "Just one thing before you go, Tony. You double-cross me, you'll wish you'd never been born. You got my word on it!" And the door closed.

There was about twenty seconds of silence. I was thinking the CD was over when someone started laughing.

"Nice one, boss!" Another few seconds passed and the same door, or another, opened. There were footsteps and a female said,

"Sounds like you're back in the Freemont."

"Certainly looks that way, Davina doll!"

I made myself a cup of coffee and played it again. I wondered about Jack. To tell or not to tell. That was the question!

CHAPTER 31

I was still thinking about the answer when the phone rang again. It was a breathless, panicky Zoe. She didn't even say hello.

"I've had an anonymous letter threatening me."

"What did it say?"

"'If we don't get it, Tony dies. Then you.'"

"When was this?"

"Don't know. I was just on my way out and saw it by the door. Never mind when it arrived. What about me? What the fuck have I got to do with anything?"

"You tell me! You still got it?"

"No. I sent it to the *Antiques Road Show*. Of course, I've still got it!"

"I'm coming over."

"Oh, one other thing. Lenny Jordan's dead!"

"How? When?"

"Last night in hospital."

"How d'you know?"

"From Ricky. What's an embolism?"

"Blood clot."

"One of those in his heart. It went from his hands or arm or something. Apparently someone nailed him to a wall."

She didn't sound upset. Neither was I for that matter.

I wondered if he'd had time to speak to anyone about me. If not, no one knew I had the CD. If yes. Danny would be looking for me.

She buzzed me in. She wore a green singlet and a grey mini and mules that clicked on the parquet and enough Miss D'Ore to stir my juices. I remembered the smell on Tony's sheets and pillowcases and a mental image of them at it in bed flashed through my mind again.

"Here!" she said, without a 'hello'. It was an ordinary A4 sheet of photocopy paper that you could buy in a million stationers. The words were cut from a magazine and gummed on.

"Well?"

"I just don't get it."

"Great!" She flopped onto the settee and lit up. "Like scaring me shitless wasn't enough!" She took a long drag, closed her eyes and exhaled. Took another and asked if I wanted a drink.

"Too early."

"Well, it must be six o'clock somewhere in the world!" and poured herself a Scotch and American.

I reread the letter and said,

"I just don't get it."

The drink calmed her. Her speech slowed, her body language relaxed. There was even a smile.

"Please, sit down. Sorry, I should have more manners" and she patted the vacant part of the settee. She half-turned to face me, running circles of her magenta-coloured hair around a finger. "I thought you might have some answers, Eddie. You were so cool and together the other day." She pointed to the letter and said, "Does this mean Jack doesn't have the money?"

"Money?"

"For the ransom."

"Jack's got money."

"The note sounds a little desperate, don't you think?"

"Desperate? Why would they be? They're holding all the cards. And why involve you?"

She shuffled a few inches closer and in so doing, spilt some of the drink on my trousers.

"Oh, shit! I'm such a clumsy cow." She went into the kitchen and came back with a damp cloth and began dabbing.

"It's okay," I said.

"No, let me. I insist." She leaned over. I could smell the perfume from her neck, her throat. The singlet hid hardly anything. Bare shoulders, bare neck. And if you cared to look down the front of it, which I did, it showed there was nothing holding up the boobs except youth and good genes. She must have known I was looking. But it didn't seem to bother her.

"There!" she said, looking up at me.

"You're a dab hand at this, aren't you?"

"Dab hand? At what exactly?"

"Dabbing."

"Oh, dabbing. What were we talking about?"

"Can't remember."

"The ransom. Maybe it's not money after all. What d'you think? Perhaps if you tell me what you know, I can help fill in a few blanks. I do want to help. He is my boyfriend after all's said and done."

"What makes you think it might not be money, Zoe?"

"Something you said the other day about a book."

"Not me."

"Yes. You asked me if this Collette bitch had mentioned one."

"Did I?"

"Is that the ransom? Does Jack have a book that's to be swapped for Tony?" She squeezed the cloth releasing droplets of water and rubbed it on the trousers, then slowly smoothed the crease it left with her hand, very slowly moving it wider and wider than the area of the spillage. "That's it, isn't it?"

"Ransom is usually about money."

"Come on. I only want to help. How are the trousers?"

"They'll dry."

"Good. Wouldn't want to send you home wet." She moved closer, her face inches from me. Her voice lower, huskier. "Talking of wet. Eddie. Did it turn you on telling you what happened? A woman stripping me, then touching me wherever she wanted. And me not able to stop her because I'm handcuffed around a beam. Did it? You know, I thought she might even strip herself she was enjoying fondling me so much, female flesh pressed against female flesh. Boobs squashed against boobs and all that. Did it? Because I know guys find it very horny two women with their hands over each other, then slowly, very slowly, sliding them between each other's legs, then slipping their long warm fingers inside one another getting each hotter and hotter, especially if it's two fingers at a time."

I could feel my heart racing. Then blood pumping at my temples. A film of sweat broke on my upper lip. She could see what she was doing. But she just sat there looking, letting my own imagination do the work for her.

"Did it? I bet it did!" She slipped her hand off my thigh and between my legs. "Jesus! It certainly did, didn't it! That feels like a serious piece of equipment, Sutton."

"Does it?"

"It most certainly does! And so cramped."

She unzipped my trousers. Out it came. And down she went, bringing a whole new meaning to the phrase paying lip service. She began licking, then licking with the underside of her tongue. She looked up and asked me to let her know if I was going to come. And then she went back to work, slowly, methodically, with a damp warm mouth sucking the sanity out of me. She undid my trousers and pulled them free, then my boxers. Then pulled off her singlet.

"No point peeping, when you can get a proper look, is there." And the look was well worthwhile. They were small but firm and round with large brown areolae and round nipples.

I pulled her skirt down, then her knickers. She had hardly any pubic hair. She saw me looking and said Tony liked her shaved. She took my hand and slipped it between her thighs.

"D'you like me shaved?"

"I'll have you however you come." Which was on her bed face down on her knees and forearms. I grabbed her by her hair pulling her towards me.

"Harder! Harder!" she kept saying. "Harder" and kept rocking back and forth trying to take me further into her.

I was hard at it, if you'll pardon the phrase, thrusting for all I was worth. She kept saying,

"I like it hard and rough. Come on, fuck me, fuck me! Fuck me!"

So I grabbed that beautiful arse and just kept ramming. And then her breathing changed, heavier, faster. I could feel her building, building, building. Close, closer, and then the wave finally hit the shore. She began shaking. Her fingers tore at her hair as she shrieked obscenities,

"Jesus, fuck! Jesus fucking Christ! Fucking hell! What a cock! You're a fuck and a half, Sutton! A fuck and a half!" But I just kept at it until finally I was done and then I collapsed beside her. She turned over and lay there eyes closed. "Oooooh, that was nice. Nice! Nice! Nice! You've done this before."

"Once or twice. But practice makes perfect."

"Pass me some tissues." I did from a box on her bedside table. "Oh, I wouldn't worry about not being perfect. That," she said, pointing, "should be photographed, the photo framed and hung in a gallery some place entitled *Eighth Wonder of the World*." She rolled over, resting her head on her hands. "I can see definite benefits working with you, Eddie."

It was then I noticed bruising at the top of her thigh, just beneath the buttock. Oval-shaped the size of a walnut. The outer area yellowy brown. The middle still mauvish, red. I ran my finger around the outline.

"Does it hurt?"

"What we talking about?"

"The bruising. I thought you said Collette hadn't actually hit you."

"It's no big deal!"

"So she did."

"No."

"It looks nasty. How d'you get it?"

"It's really no big deal!"

"How?"

"It, it, it was Tony, if you must know. We had an argument one night and he kicked me a couple of times. It was probably my fault for starting it."

She looked so sexy, sweating, her hair in a mess, and the smell of perfume exuding from practically every pore. But underneath it all, she struck me as nothing more than all packaging and no substance.

"He said he was sorry. It wouldn't happen again."

"Has he done it before?"

"He said he was sorry. Okay! Now, let it go. Talk about picking your moments for twenty questions!"

"Let's hope someone's good with the leg make-up."

"Come again!"

"For your photo shoots. I saw one of you." She smiled. But it was just vanity. "A lads' mag."

"A girl's gotta earn the rent. Which one?"

"*Hot and Wet*."

"Don't know it."

"One of Leon Doorrell's top-shelf publications."

The smile faded.

"Leon Doorrell? You've lost me. Never heard of him. You must have me confused with someone else. Or someone looking like me. I want a drink," she suddenly said. "What about you?"

"Coffee'll do." She slid off the bed, into a pair of knickers and T-shirt.

"White or black?"

"White," and remembering what her coffee tasted like added, "Strong!"

I waited a few moments then went through her bedside drawer. I don't know why. Maybe it was just the nosy bastard gene in me at work. Or maybe I thought I might find something to understand why she was screwing me. I wasn't expecting to find anything of importance. And that's what I found. The best way of searching a place is when it's empty. Then you have time to go through things. Read bits of paper, letters that may be important, peruse diaries. It occurred to me to come back one night when she was at work. It wouldn't be hard for me to get in. The street door had a regular deadlock and Yale you could do with a pick and a large square piece of plastic. It's not hard if you know what you're doing. I always thought if I hadn't been a copper I would have made quite a competent villain.

There was a dressing table across the room by a window. Perfume bottles, a framed photo of Tony. One of an older couple, her parents perhaps, and one of a man in his twenties in army uniform, perhaps a brother. It had two drawers, bras, knickers, tights. There was a walk-in wardrobe. Clothes, clothes, clothes, and handbags and at the bottom a shoe rack with enough shoes to have made Imelda Marcos envious.

"Sugar?" she called.

"Oh, yeah!" I went into the living room and put on my clothes. "Can I use your loo?"

"First on the right!"

I had a pee and checked her medicine cabinet. It contained what you'd expect of a horny, over-sexed, good-looking 25-year-old female. Blister packs of the Pill, shampoos, conditioner, face cream, moisturiser, cotton buds, disposable razors. I went back into the living room. She had her back to me making coffee. There was a room unit against a far wall at the other end from the kitchen. Its shelves dressed with photos, books, a CD rack, plumbed-in hi-fi. I was sliding open a drawer when she said, "Come and get it!"

She asked if the coffee was okay. But it wasn't.

"Nice," I said. But it was as bad as the first time.

She was leaning against the sink unit, her hands around a mug. She looked good in T-shirt and knickers and knowing what there was underneath I was tempted to take her back into the bedroom.

"Must be autosuggestion," she said.

"What?"

"Using the loo. Back in a trice!"

I made a quick search of the kitchen cupboards. Crockery, utensils, foodstuffs, cereal boxes, coffee, tea, sugar, crackers. There was a fridge full of yogurts, orange juice, eggs, cheese, a few ready-made meal cartons. I took my coffee into the living room and slid open a drawer. Bills, couple of parking tickets, credit card statements. I heard the bathroom lock turn. I shoved the lot away and sat on the settee.

"Won't be a mo!" she called.

When she came back she was in grey tracksuit bottoms and a red shirt hanging loose, and bare feet. She sat beside me and said,

"I've been thinking. We should definitely work

together on this thing, Eddie. I know I want to. What d'you reckon?"

I'd been a sole trader for four years. And then in the last twenty-four hours had had two offers of partnership. It was just like Mary said after Jesus was born. 'You wait and wait for a wise man and then three turn up together!'

"Sounds good," I replied.

"I think we'll make a great team. We're compatible in so many ways." Then she touched my lips with a finger. She found her coffee, took a couple of sips and then casually said, "I was just thinking. Does Jack have any idea who's snatched Tony?"

"None."

"Really. Not even a hunch?"

"Not a clue."

"Talking of assumptions. I'm assuming you might want to see me again socially?"

"Hmmm! That would be nice."

"In the meantime, I'll ask around the club, discreetly, of course, see if Jack has any enemies."

"What a great idea!"

"Then maybe we can get together and exchange information. Perhaps by then you'll know what he has planned."

"Nice thinking!"

She clinked her mug against mine and toasted partnerships.

I asked her if she'd mind me borrowing the letter. She said 'no' and as she handed it to me from the coffee table, her mobile trilled in her bedroom. She went in there to answer it. I tried to listen. But she closed the door. She was back in a few minutes.

"Sorry. Got to go. That was a girlfriend; I should have been round at hers half an hour ago. Can't think what made me forget the time. Will you ring me when you know something?"

"Sure!"
"Promise? You have my number, don't you?"
"Oh yeah! I've got your number all right!"

CHAPTER 32

My head was full of Zoe dressed and undressed as I drove back to my office. I wondered how she fitted into things. Because her continual pumping for information and my seduction was no accident. I kept wondering if I'd missed anything. That maybe Danny or Doorrell were connected after all and I just couldn't see it. Or maybe it was her and Ricky's show. Or even hers and Collette's. Perhaps Collette had decided to become top dog by putting Danny behind bars and Doorrell at her mercy and scared Zoe into helping. Because I only had Zoe's word for what went on in that room while she was handcuffed around the beam. It all seemed a jumble. A kaleidoscope of possibilities. Some bizarre. Some possible. It occurred to me I needed to sit down and just think this whole thing right the way through.

And then Maxine popped into my head. Two different women in two days. Zoe was just a scalp. But Maxine was different. I felt guilty about doing it with Zoe as though I'd cheated on Maxine. Which was ridiculous because I hardly knew her. I was between relationships at the moment. The last had ended, as others, living together for a while then drifting apart because I didn't really want to commit. Your whole life changes when you're under the same roof with someone. I have single friends. We like bars and clubs because we're not short of a bob or two. We like eyeing women, even if we don't always pull. I like the impromptu decision to play cards and find myself still playing into the small hours. Bachelor stuff, no responsibilities, hard to surrender. And now I'd met a woman who'd struck a note I was unfamiliar with. Something had happened in her flat. Perhaps my adulthood had caught up with me. I looked in the driver's mirror and told the face there that I was falling for her. A voice in my head said 'no'. But it didn't sound convincing. I pulled over and dialled her.

"Hello!"

"Are you okay? You sound a little lost."

"I'm at the top of Adelaide Road."

"You know what I mean."

"How are you?"

"I told my sister about you."

"Oh dear!"

"Ssssh! D'you know what she said? She thought I'd met someone because I looked happy for the first time in ages."

I had an urge to tell her that I wished I was with her. But wondered if it might not sound mushy.

"She said she'd have liked to have met you."

"Why couldn't she stay longer?"

"Had to get back to Spain. She's suddenly such a busy girl these days, my sister. Money to sort out here. Property to deal with there. She's trying to unload a villa at the moment."

"Why, she coming back to England?"

"Oh, no! She's definitely an ex-pat. There's even less reason for her to come back now she's got money." There was a long moment of silence between us. And then she said, "What you thinking?"

"How glad I am that we met." But it wasn't the only thing going through my mind. What was also, was how to subtly get her DOB.

"Want to know a secret?"

"Go on!"

"Cross your heart, promise not to tell?"

"Promise."

"So am I. Good, isn't it!"

And then a bloody traffic warden spoilt the moment by tapping on the window and signalling me to move on.

"There's a warden telling me to shove off."

"Go on, then. I'll speak to you later." I was about to click off when she said, "Eh, Mister Sutton. Haven't you forgotten something?" And I blew her a kiss.

I got back to my office and clicked my answerphone for messages. There was a few seconds of stifled giggling, then a voice said,

"I am Svetlana from Russian embassy. I am after your body." It was Maxine in an iffy Soviet accent. "I have plans to kidnap you and keep you as my personal sex toy and have you obey my many daily demands." There was a pause, more giggling, then, "You haf bin varned!" I played it again and laughed. Played it again and laughed again. The next message was from a possible new client wanting to fix an appointment. Then someone flogging double glazing. And then I stopped in my tracks as the thought hit me from out of nowhere. Tony's box of Omeprazole for his ulcer was no longer in Zoe's flat! I told myself that perhaps I'd missed it. But I knew I hadn't. Then I told myself she may have put it in her car. Why? Or taken it to the Freemont with her? Why? I rang Arnie to have him follow her for a few days instead of Ricky and see what it turned up. But he was on voicemail. Then I rang Steve.

"Can you talk?" I asked.

"Yes. What's up?"

"You once told me you had a pepper spray. Still got it?"

"Yes."

"Can I borrow it?"

"Trouble?"

"There might be a couple of geezers looking for me."

"Need help?"
"Maybe. Just the spray at the moment."
"Come by in the morning."
"Ta!"
"Any time!"

I used going to the Freemont to finalise arrangements regarding Davina's funeral as an excuse to see Maxine with a big bunch of roses.

"I had to see Jack. So I thought I'd deliver a kiss at the same time."

"Where do I sign for it?"

"Just here." And I pointed to my lips.

She smelt the flowers and said she'd get someone to put them in water. But later. She came into my arms. I felt her body through her thin white shirt, soft, warm, engaging. She wore the same perfume as in the restaurant, sharp with something of a punch. But classy, making her smell so incredibly sexy that the hydraulics began to stir. She kissed me hard, then stuck her tongue in my ear sending a nice shiver through me.

"I've been thinking about you, Sutton. I seem to be thinking about you quite a lot as it happens!" she said, undoing my shirt buttons and kissing my chest.

"About anything in particular?"

"Oh, yeah! Is the door closed?" I checked it was. "Lock it!" She pulled my jacket off and undid my trouser belt, then unzipped me. "I want you right now!"

I unfastened her shirt, bra, skirt. She kicked them all away together with her panties. And I took her up against the wall with her arms around my neck and her legs around my waist. And we went at it.

"Oooooh, Eddie, Eddie darling! You just don't know what's happening to me!" I did. Because it was happening to me. But I was too full of lust and thrust for a conversation. She tightened her grip around me. I began pushing harder and harder. "Oh, it's so good having you inside me, baby. So, so good!" she moaned. She bit my neck and licked the blood. "I just want to eat you up, Sutton!"

My response was to penetrate harder and further and she closed her eyes as the pleasure consumed her.

I carried her over to her desk sweeping, everything off it with an arm. She draped herself across it. We picked up a rhythm not like the recently acquainted having a quick fuck. But like familiar lovers with passion who knew each other's moves, likes and dislikes. I could smell the sweat and perfume as her body became hotter and hotter from all the shaking and rocking as we continued like a pair of animals.

"Oh, Eddie, Eddie!" she moaned. "Oh, it's just so, so good!" She wriggled that lovely pink arse, getting me even harder if that was possible. And then her tone changed. The moaning was more stifled, her eyes closed, she began shaking, the shudder reverberating throughout her body. Then she came. "Aaaaah! You don't know what you do to me! You just don't know what you do to me, baby!"

She gathered up her clothes, dressed, picked up the telephone, the intercom, some papers and the flowers and put them on her desk. She lay back in her office chair, hands on her head, watching me dress.

"I was going to have a coffee break as you arrived. But I've got to tell you. This was a whole lot better." She blew me a kiss and said, "I'm really glad that we met you know, and not just because of …!"

I finished dressing and looked up at her.

"So am I."

"Are you?"

"Oh, yeah. Sometimes I find it hard to say things. I want to speak what's on my mind. But the words kind of get stuck inside me." Like, I wanted to say, I couldn't believe how lucky I'd got. Because I'd never met anyone like her. She ticked all the boxes. Good-looking, sexy, brains, funny.

"What's stuck there at the moment?" she asked.

"That, that, that, that I am really glad we met. Maybe more than I'd care to admit to."

"I hope so," she said, picking up a single stem that had become detached from the bunch and slowly arrowed it towards me. "Because I'm getting hooked on you, Sutton."

Someone knocked, then tried the door handle. She ran her hands over her hair, then smoothed her skirt and turned the key. Jack stood framed in the doorway.

"Damn door!" she exclaimed. "It keeps jamming. I keep meaning to ring maintenance." He came into the room and looked around. "Eddie bought me some flowers. Wasn't that nice of him." She smelt them as though I'd just arrived.

He gave me a look as though not quite sure whether flowers were the only thing she'd had from me.

"Reception said you were here. Maybe we could have a word in my office. If you can tear yourself away."

"Of course!"

"I've decided to go to the funeral from my house instead of Sybil's."

I followed him out. Was at the door and turned back to Maxine, whose face was just one big smile and then she slowly, seductively, pursed her lips and blew me a silent kiss.

"Maybe we could continue our chat later," I said.

"I look forward to it. Although I did get the thrust of what was on your mind!"

CHAPTER 33

Bushy Jewish Cemetery was two or three miles from Stanmore. An up-market middle-class suburb of North West London. It was off a long semi-rural lane. Nicely kept houses and bungalows one side. Open land opposite.

Jack insisted we all travel together. Me and him in the back of the Jag, Terry driving.

"You expecting any aggro, guv?" Terry asked.

"Danny'll be there. He'll have a minder with him. Perhaps two. So be ready for anything."

"Stafford'll be there as well," I said.

"The copper?"

"Has he called again?" I asked.

"The other day. Said Tony was now prime suspect for Davina's murder. He wanted his mobile number. Practically called me a liar when I told him I didn't have it. My house is being watched. So is the club. Like I don't have enough problems."

He gave a deep sigh and slumped right back in the leather upholstery.

"Why haven't the kidnappers called? That's what I want to know. It's been two days now. Two days! That's not good. You don't think …?"

"No, I don't. They need him alive."

"Once he's back, at least we'll have him to get the law off our case."

"You hope!"

He turned to me and asked angrily what I meant by that.

"Let's pray Tony can give them some right answers, "I

said.

"You mean about Davina's death?"

"Her last call was from him. And I understand there was bad blood between them."

"Rubbish!"

Terry turned right through two large iron gates.

"Here we go, guv!"

The roadway curved. We stopped momentarily in front of a wide paved and canopied walkway affording access and entry to the prayer hall, a building of a large light coloured concrete structure with big wooden double doors. It was set amongst greenery with attractive well-kept sixty-foot sycamores either side.

Jack lowered his window and eyed the people milling around the entrance. They seemed mainly middle-aged and though they'd come to a funeral were convivial with each other. They all looked well turned out. The women in dark dresses and hats or headscarves. The men in suits with black or dark-coloured ties. There was a younger element nearer the door, thirty-somethings. The men less formal than their elders, in trousers and jackets rather than suits. The women, some in shirts and skirts covered by ponchos.

I told Terry to drive a few hundred feet to a designated parking area opposite a small terrace of single-storey structures which I guessed were admin offices.

"Danny's here," I said.

"Where?" Jack looked around. "You must have eyes like a bloody hawk. Where?"

"In the four by four to your left."

There was a minder and a driver in front and Danny in the back, playing with a mobile or a game. Opposite but a little further on Stafford in an unmarked two-door red Hyundai. He sat beside a man, perhaps a DC. I wondered if he'd disrespect the occasion by snapping faces. I told Terry my guess was he'd leave the DC behind to amble over later to start a conversation and pump him.

"He can try!"

Jack got out of the car. Stafford out of his.

"Mister Kreeger. Eddie!" Stafford said. He donned a trilby, brown felt with a dark brown petersham band; it made him look distinguished. "Unfortunate circumstances to meet at."

"Very."

"Thought I'd pay my respects as I'm still investigating." He fiddled with the hat as if he wasn't used to wearing one. Then checked his tie knot. "I wonder if your Tony will turn up, seeing he was a friend of Miss Miller's."

Jack shrugged.

"No news from him yet?"

"None." Jack replied.

"Must be enjoying Bournemouth, or wherever he is. You did say he was in Bournemouth, didn't you?"

"Yes."

"Hmm, Bournemouth, that's right. We can't seem to locate him there. And we really would like to speak to him. I understand the late Mrs Kreeger has a sister in Florida."

"Yes, Dora."

"And you've got first cousins in Los Angeles?" Jack nodded. "Also nice places for a holiday. Unless you prefer Bournemouth, of course!"

"I wouldn't know. I've never been to Bournemouth. If you'll excuse me, I want to pay my condolences to the bereaved. Eddie?"

"I'll be along in a minute, Jack."

"Tough little bastard, isn't he," Stafford said, watching Jack, hands in jacket pockets, walking towards the prayer hall entrance.

"He lives in a tough world."

"Don't we all!"

I fell into step with Stafford. We'd gone a few yards when he said, "Ever been to a Jewish funeral ?"

"No."

"They're an amazing people, the Jews. They have a thing called a shiva after the internment. It means seven in Hebrew. The immediate bereaved sit for seven days in low chairs during the waking hours at someone's house trying to come to terms with their grief and loss."

The wind blew. I managed to trap the skull cap Jack had given me before it flew off.

"Sounds a bit morbid to me."

"I don't know. What do we do? Have a wake. Get smashed. Wake up the next morning with a hangover, still confronted with the grief. Their laws are five thousand years old. Interesting how it straddles modern psychiatry about confronting stuff instead of denying it. There's a lot to be said for confronting what you'd rather deny or suppress. Wouldn't you say?" he said, watching Jack approach some people.

"I guess. How d'you know all this stuff?"

"My sister-in-law's Jewish." We walked on another few yards. He suddenly put a hand on my arm. "D'you speak to Jack about Tony's whereabouts?"

"He keeps insisting he's in Bournemouth."

"Yeah, right! You met this Maxine Andrews that works for Jack?"

"Yes. What of it?"

"That's presumably the Andrews you wanted checked out?"

"Yes. You able to without a date of birth?"

"I'll see what I can do. I had a word with her."

"And?"

"I reckon I could get more conversation out of people

on life-support machines. She's hiding something. It wouldn't surprise me if her and Tony are having it off. And that's where he is right now. Underneath her duvet waiting for her come home."

I was about to tell him that it was unlikely when he said,

"Thanks for the heads up on Newcastle by the way! Looks like we may have nailed a couple of Carlin's suppliers."

"And this Birmingham thing regarding money Davina might owe?"

"I don't think we're going to need to pursue it."

"Because?"

"Between you, me and the gravestones?"

"Go on."

"We picked up a registration number off the red Ferrari from the street CCTV I mentioned the other day. It was Tony's car. And our blokes got an image off the video entryphone. Young Tony looked pissed off enough to have chewed his way through Davina Miller's expensive Axminster carpets. All we need now is to confirm his DNA on her face and that's another crime solved by Chelsea and Westminster's finest!" He pulled on my arm and swung me round so that we were eyeball to eyeball. "Sooner or later I'm going to get my hands on that little fucker! You can make book on it!"

CHAPTER 34

The interior of the prayer hall was about forty feet long, with a natural brickwork finish with large hexagonal-shaped windows set high up admitting some sunshine. So the hall was half in light, half in shadow. The floor was white stone. In the middle was a lectern and beside it a coffin upon a bier covered with a black cloth. There was a pair of large double doors through which everyone entered and another set at the other end of the hall. Forty or so people. The men stood against the left-hand side wall. The women against the right.

There were two mourners seated on chairs close to the coffin. Davina's mother, slim, in her sixties, with large brown eyes, now red-rimmed. She had a small nose, blond hair tucked underneath a black headscarf. Her face, pasty-white, looking shell-shocked. And her son, Norman. Tall, thin. Bald with horn-rimmed specs. He sat holding her hand.

I stood beside Stafford, who was busy clocking faces. One of them Danny's. I looked his way. He looked mine. His vacant expression didn't change. I wondered if he knew about the CD. I supposed it depended on whether he'd caught up with Jordan before he'd snuffed it. And if he had would he would try something here? I tapped my jacket pocket and felt the outline of the pepper spray. Funeral or not, any trouble, I'd made up my mind. I'd do him and his minders. He went back to staring at the coffin transfixed. Someone handed him a prayer book. He took it, without averting his gaze. Someone handed me a book.

Not far from him was Ricky Houston. He stared briefly at the coffin, then caught my eye and nodded. Then started leafing through the pages. We were all directed to page one by the rabbi waiting to conduct the service.

The usher in black suit and top hat was just closing the doors when Collette squeezed through them, and joined the women. She mouthed a 'hello' to Ricky. I wondered for a moment how she knew him. Then guessed from gambling at the tables for Danny. She caught his eye as well and mouthed another 'hello'. I wondered what would happen if Zoe showed up. It didn't bear thinking about. So I didn't. Then she caught my eye. It took her a second or two to download me. Customer, victim, friend of Danny's. Then it registered. She tried to outstare me. But couldn't. Though every so often she'd look my way and find me still looking.

The rabbi read some prayers. Then invited Norman to deliver a eulogy. He stepped up to the lectern. There were no notes. No prompt cards. Whatever he had to say was going to come from his heart and his guts. And it did. He spoke in a cracked voice about a loving devoted daughter, loving sister and that his vocabulary and command of the English language were insufficient to express how much he would miss her. He mentioned a few family anecdotes. One about when she was twelve and he fifteen. He'd asked her to get him a red-and-black-striped ink biro while she was out. The shopkeeper had obviously told her that it was a wind-up. So she bought a can of Sprite out of his money and poured it down the back of his shirt, which had resulted in a cushion fight. He stopped for a moment, his voice now really shaky. He clenched a fist to stop himself from breaking down altogether. Then he went on to talk about her as an adult and her amazing business acumen.

And there they were all the platitudes, however well

meant, that you hear when someone dies. Shame nobody thinks to mention them to the deceased when they're alive. When such compliments and kindness might do some good and in the case of Davina perhaps have given her something more than coke to lean on.

The rabbi invited the congregation to follow the coffin for the burial. It was wheeled through the other pair of doors and along a concrete path past rows of headstones, some in white marble with black writing, others in grey marble with white or gold writing.

We ambled in a snake of forty or so people behind it, and Sybil and Norman. A breeze riffled the branches of surrounding trees. Some birds flew west towards the sun. Across to my left Danny and Collette exchanged words. They looked over at me and Stafford. Then Collette put a finger to her lips and nodded. And the contradiction struck me. Such evil in a place of such holiness.

We assembled at the grave. The excavated earth piled beside it thick and damp and sprinkled with small stones. The men stood one side. The women the other. The coffin was lowered. Sybil let out a long low wail into a tissue, then convulsed with tears. A woman not dissimilar in looks, a sister perhaps, put her arms around her and kissed the crown of her head. But it didn't help.

The rabbi recited something. I asked Stafford in a whisper how long the internment took. He shrugged, and said,

"Until they run out of prayers, I suppose."

I eased my way over to Jack.

"You okay?" I asked.

"What a waste," he sighed, "they should bring back hanging!"

A shovel was handed to Norman, who threw a few spadefuls of earth into the grave; they landed with a dull thud, the stones bounced, then he handed the shovel to an older man behind him, who did the same then handed the shovel on to someone else.

"What's all that about Jack?" I asked.

"Tradition! The last thing you can do for someone is to help bury them." He shovelled some himself, then handed me the spade.

I threw some earth on the casket. It seemed to me such a traumatic way to say goodbye to someone. But then who am I to tell people what they should or should not do, especially if they have been doing it for the last five thousand years. Then it occurred to me helping to bury someone is the first step in coming to terms with the loss. So maybe the Jews have it right after all! When the last man had finished, the gravediggers filled in the rest.

We reassembled in the prayer hall, resuming our former places. The rabbi said a few more prayers. Then Norman was invited to say Kaddish, the prayer for the dead. People closed their books, the tension in the hall eased. He resumed his place on the chair beside his mother and everyone filed past, shaking hands with them, wishing both a long life. It was over. Such a dignified funeral for such an undignified death. I looked around for Danny and Collette, expecting trouble. But they were already at the exit. Ricky was chatting to some people, friends of Davina's perhaps.

Stafford's DC was waiting for him outside the prayer hall and walked him towards their motor. He came abreast of us and said he hoped to hear from Tony soon. And he and the DC took off.

The sun had cut through the clouds shining brightly on the car. That's why I didn't notice it immediately. A white A4 envelope spiked on the Jag's aerial. My first thought was that it was an advertising flyer. My second that that would have been left under the wipers. I pulled it off. It was addressed to Jack, so I handed it him. He looked quizzically at me then at the envelope, then tore it open and a gold ring fell out of it. He picked it up, looked at it and said,

"Tony's signet ring. Here; look. His initials, AK." He read the note with it. It was an A4 sheet with words gummed to it, exactly like Zoe's. He read it again. Then handed it to me.

> TOMORROW NOON, LEAVE MILLER'S BOOK AT LEFT LUGGAGE OFFICE, LIVERPOOL STREET STATION. LEAVE RECEIPT SLIPPED BETWEEN TRAIN DEPARTURE TIME TABLE FRAME OPPOSITE. THEN LEAVE. YOU WILL BE WATCHED. ANY TRICKS, YOUR SON DIES.

The colour had drained from his face. His brow became heavily corrugated. He took the letter back and reread it, then read it a fourth time. Then just stood there staring at it.

"Taking the piss, isn't it!" he said at last.

"How d'you mean?"

"Leaving a ransom note at a funeral. All we need now is fog instead of sunshine and it could be right out of a fucking Hollywood film!"

I looked around for CCTV cameras. But there weren't any.

"How'd it go, guv?" Terry asked, ambling over. "Everything all right?"

"No, it's bloody not! Where have you been?"

"Why?"

"Where?"

"Taking a pee! Why, what's happened?"

"This!" And Jack shoved the letter at him.

"Sorry, guv. I wasn't to know how long the service would be." He read the letter. Took off his cap and wiped his forehead with a shirtsleeve.

"How long?"

"Five, six minutes."

"You see anyone hanging around the car?"

Terry shook his head.

"You were right, Sutton," Terry said. "The other copper tried to chat me. Saw he wasn't getting anywhere and sat outside the prayer hall chapel thing. Then I went off…"

Jack yanked open the car door, slumped in the back seat and shouted,

"Get me out of here!"

We drove back to Hampstead in absolute silence. Him looking out of the window biting a thumbnail. Me trying to make sense of it all. He was right. It was like taking the piss. But by whom? Ricky? Zoe? Then the late arrival of Collette popped into my head. It gave her the opportunity. Jack and I sat in the library. The sun had followed us. It streamed through the dome-topped windows, leaving shafts across his desk. He sat spinning his glasses case.

"Hmm!" he said at last.

"Well, now we know why they waited."

"We do?" he said, smashing a fist down on the case and sending it spinning across the room.

"So they didn't have to speak to you."

"They could have posted it."

"Risky. It might have got lost. How would they address it? With cut-out letters? That would just about put the shits up everyone in a sorting office."

"Drink?"

"Oh, yeah."

He poured Scotch. I told him to make it a double. I took a long belt of it and on an empty stomach the effect was a treat. I told him I'd get to Liverpool Street with Terry at 11 a.m. He, Jack, was to get there at noon. Leave the book. Plant the receipt, then go home.

"Then what?" he asked.

'Once Tony's safely back home, he gets arrested for murder' is what I wanted to say. But instead I said, "I follow the book. Terry follows A. N. Other if there's more than one." I kept wondering who knew Jack would be at the funeral. All the players did. But not all the players had been there.

"What you thinking?" he asked.

"That I wish I'd been on holiday when you first rang!"

CHAPTER 35

Kilburn was no more than fifteen minutes' drive from Jack. So I decided to drop in on Steve. He'd had a huge plasma screen installed and instead of people playing, a lot were huddled around it watching Spurs taking a thrashing from the Gunners, as is how things should be.

"Since when?"

"Two days ago. The playing's down. But the drinking's up." He plonked a half in front of me. "You could have rung instead of coming in. It wasn't that necessary."

"Why?"

"Why? Checked your messages lately?"

"No. I've been busy. What's up?"

"I called. I had the cops in here."

"Because?"

"Arnie's dead!"

"Jesus! How? When? Accident?"

"No accident, mate. Murder."

"Bloody hell!"

"They reckon electrocuted."

"What!"

He told me how some night shift workers repairing roads in King's Cross had found his naked body wrapped in polythene dumped in one of the arches.

"Poor sad little Arnie! I hardly knew him. But you know I feel quite bad."

"It gets worse." He looked up and down the counter to make sure he was out of earshot. "His clothes were found a few yards away. Probably thrown from the car or van that dumped him. The cops found a mobile in his jacket."

"Don't tell me. It had your number listed."

"And yours!"

"Shit!"

"You're going to get a visit. You best have a story ready. And make sure that pepper spray's well hidden." He seemed more engaged with me now he'd told me. Then said how he'd told the cops Arnie used to do casual work for him and that's why he had his number. "Who'd want to kill a poor little sod like that?"

"A bitch called Collette Hammond," I replied.

"You know who did it?"

"The MO fits. She works for Carlin. I think Arnie was probably in the wrong place at the wrong moment." And that was because of me, giving him a few quid to follow someone.

I took a sip of my beer. It suddenly didn't taste so good. Poor little Arnie. I'd told him to scram when he told me about Carlin's men. He probably looked a bit too nosy and they'd grabbed him. Hence the abandoned moped. And then she'd gone to work on him. But this time a bit too far. Murder or manslaughter. He was dead because of me. I sat there, my hands on my forehead, looking at the drink but not seeing anything. So what now? I tried to think things through. Carlin's men would have gone to Ricky. He'd have persuaded them he didn't have the CD, otherwise he wouldn't have had two working legs to go to Davina's funeral with. They'd have gone back to Jordan, who must have been taken to hospital by then. So it all depended whether they'd got to him in hospital. My guess was no. Which meant no one knew I had the CD. My thoughts went back to Arnie. Poor little Arnie. He must have been scared shitless! And then a picture of Collette mincing into the prayer hall popped into my head. The sick bitch commits murder, then goes to a funeral. I promised myself, however this affair ended, she'd hear from me.

CHAPTER 36

I opened my flat door and there she stood in a navy denim skirt and red check shirt. Her hair centre-parted and swept to the sides and held there with a gold-coloured slide and pin. The eyes Wedgwood blue, sparkling, full lips with lipstick just right. A picture just so pleasing on the eye. She produced a large glass bowl of tiramisu from behind her back.

"Made in Notting Hill. With just one customer in mind!"

"Looks good enough to eat."

"So do you." She pecked my cheek and asked where the kitchen was. She opened the door and took a deep breath. "Something smells good."

I kissed her neck.

"Certainly does!"

She put the bowl on the worktop then her arms around me.

"So, Mister Sutton. How are we today?"

"All the better for seeing you."

"You're to hold that thought at all times."

We kissed and I realised how much I liked being with her and how much I missed her when I wasn't. And how she was feeling like a dimension to my life.

"The food smells yummy. What we having?"

"Fettuccine with home-made pesto, garlic, pine nuts and mushrooms. But to start with – avocado salad with tomato, rocket and the Sutton special sauce. The recipe is a family secret."

"Really!"

"Yes. Not my family's. It's the deli owner's secret where I buy my stuff. So if you don't like it, blame him."

"Can I help?"

"No. Just sit on a kitchen stool and continue to look gorgeous."

We sat at a candlelit table I'd given the works with linen tablecloth and napkins, gleaming cutlery, perfectly laid. Water, soft drinks, bread in a small wicker basket and Amy Whitehouse in the background, low and melodic.

"This is delicious, Eddie. Absolutely delicious."

I poured her a soft drink and went into the kitchen for a glass of wine, not wanting to leave the bottle on the table.

"We've had an invitation," she said between mouthfuls.

"That's nice."

"From Carole and her boyfriend to go see them."

"In Spain?"

"I phoned her to see that she'd got home okay. We were discussing you. And she said she and Gregg would love to meet you."

"Gregg?"

"Her boyfriend. He's a bit younger than us. But you'll like him. He's really nice. Great sense of humour."

"How young?"

"Twenty-eight."

"And Carole must be …?"

"Forty-one."

"What was he, a mature student of hers?"

"Student?"

"She was a teacher, wasn't she?" I said, remembering what Jack had said about Ronnie's girlfriend.

"Teacher! Where d'you get that from?" She explained that Carole had been an IT technician. And Gregg had sold coffee futures in the city. "He must have liked what she did with his hard drive," she continued, "because he decided his best futures deal was with her. The next thing you know, they've gone to Spain and opened a bar."

"Really. And?"

"Doing very well. They're about to open a second. That's why she was over here. To tie up finance with their bank."

It felt as though a large stone had been removed from my chest and regular breathing resumed. And as though to underline it, I found myself taking a deep breath.

"Why you staring at me like that?" she asked.

"You mean apart from being good-looking, hot and sexy, and great company?"

"Yes. Apart from that."

"I suppose I must just like looking at you."

She shuffled her chair closer.

"That's okay then. Because I like looking at you. Quite a lot actually." She ran a finger down my cheek and just stared. "How d'you get to be so handsome, Sutton?"

"I went to FACES-R-US."

We finished the meal and sat on the settee with coffee, having decided to delay dessert. The candlelight cast shadows silhouetting us on the far wall. I kissed her and she tasted good. I held her close and she felt good. And then she turned serious saying there was something on her mind. I wondered what was coming. I downloaded possibles. 'A dear Eddie.' An admission of something.

"I know we've only really just got started, Eddie. So this is going to sound, well, maybe OTT. But …"

"But?"

"If you ever want to end things, just tell me straight. Don't play games with me, okay?"

"Why would I want to end it? Where else am I going to

get coffee like you make?"

She took my head between her hands and said,

"I mean it. Straight from the shoulder. Don't spoil this with lies. She let go of me and said, "And now you're probably thinking I'm some kind of nutter. But there! I've said what I wanted to say."

"You may want to end things first."

"Unlikely!"

"How d'you know?"

"Because I do. Because … Just let's say, … because … Just let's say because I know."

"Have you never been wrong about anything?" I asked.

"Not as far as I can remember," she replied with a faint smile.

"Well, I can't see myself ending things because … The thing is … Is that … Is that. The thing is …" I sat there for a few moments like an idiot with my mouth open. "It's because … Well, the thing is … What I'm trying to say is …" And then out it came. "I love you, Maxine." And then I shrugged, a little embarrassed. "What can I say! I love you!" It felt for a moment as if someone else in the room, secreted in the shadows, had said it. Not me. Then it dawned on me it was me. And I meant it.

She gave me a long hard stare. Then she said,

"You mean it, don't you?"

She tried to blink back tears but couldn't. She closed her eyes and they ran down her cheeks into her mouth. She wiped them away and began smiling and crying at the same time, then moved up close to me. So close I could feel her breath on my face.

"Well, there's a coincidence," she finally whispered.

I had this tremendous urge just to hold her. She was so soft and warm and kissable, I just wanted to take her in my arms and never let go. I wasn't thinking about sex. Well, not then, anyway. I suppose love puts you in touch with far corners of yourself you didn't even know existed.

"What's the matter?" I asked.

"I'm just so happy."

So happy she was in a constant flood of tears. Women! Go figure!

She touched my face, and it was a new kind of touch. The soft warm hands were the same. But there was a subliminal message in the connection of skin on skin.

"When did you first realise you loved me?" she asked.

There was a ten-dollar answer and a five-dollar answer. The ten-dollar one was on the way home from Zoe. So I opted for the five-dollar version. Which wasn't altogether a lie. More a flexible interpretation of the truth.

"When I was in Adelaide Road."

"Maybe one day they'll put a plaque outside where you parked." She kissed me again so full on that I told her I could taste her lipstick. "What does it taste like?"

"Creamy, but a little astringent too."

"The cream is for love. The astringent is for lust."

"You're quite the poet."

She took my hand and put it on her breasts.

"Well, you're always telling me how much you like my twin couplets!" She massaged them with my hand. "I would be right in thinking that, wouldn't I?" I nodded like a zombie. "Good, very good. Because it's all for you."

I told her she looked tired and perhaps she should lie down. She put a finger to her temple in feigned thought and said,

"But where? That's the question."

"Let me think. Oh! I know. What about my bed?"

"Gosh! You are clever Eddie. Why didn't I think of that?"

It was a large room with magnolia-painted walls, wardrobes running the length of one side. A few prints.

The New York skyline, an abstract of a couple tangoing. Large ceiling-to-floor windows looking out onto posh Albert Street. She bounced on the bed a couple of times and said,

"I bet this could tell a few stories."

It certainly could have. It had seen enough action to complete with Blackpool beach on any night when the tide was out.

She crawled across its six-foot width, put a finger over my lips and said, "Not a word out of you, Sutton! Not a single word." Then snuggled up close and told me she loved me. "Do you love me?" she asked.

"You know I do."

"I need to hear it often. We're going to be very happy, you and me."

"Good."

"Right after you get rid of this bed."

"Why? It's a perfectly good bed," I replied as I was proposing to show her.

"It's a bit lumpy."

"Rubbish!"

"The mattress is funny."

"Not as funny as you. What's the problem?" As if I couldn't guess.

"Okay! If you must know. It's got history, hasn't it? How many women have you had in it?"

"I don't know. Four or five."

"What, dozen?"

"No, hundred!"

"Yeah, right! Not even in your dreams, Sutton! Well, however many and I really don't want to know," she said, brushing hair away from my eyes, "I bet none of them loved you as much as I do."

They hadn't. And I hadn't loved any as much as I loved her.

"Okay! I'll get rid of it. But I can't do it tonight. So we might as well give it a send-off to remember."

"Will all those in favour raise a hand and say aye," she exclaimed, and up went hers with a resounding "Motion absolutely and positively carried!"

She sat astride me. I tried to prop myself on my elbows. But she pushed me back against the pillows.

"Back. This is a leave-everything-to-Maxine evening. Because you, lover boy, are going to get well and truly laid!"

"Yes, Svetlana!"

"You won't ever forget the last tumble in this bed, Sutton. Not after I'm finished."

"Yes, Svetlana!"

"Number one. Shirt off."

By number five I hadn't a stitch on. By ten neither had she. She slid down and took me in her mouth. Slowly, precisely. But this was no routine piece of duty. This was with passion for nothing less than giving pure pleasure. It seemed to me the message was I'd never find better sex anywhere and she was probably right. Not that I was any longer interested in looking for it. Because I realised I'd found what I'd spent my entire adulthood avoiding finding. There was another message as well, which was that she'd found her man, He could have anything and she knew how to keep him.

And then she took those two little chaps in her cupped hands and started slowly, very slowly massaging them until I thought my brain would split my skull.

"How you doing, baby?" She asked. I could only grunt. "I'll take that as okay. Good, very good. Because I haven't really got started yet." And then she slipped herself right on top of me and me inside her. She began rocking back and forth her breathing becoming heavier and heavier.

Then she began gripping and releasing me. "How's that? Nice? No? Want me to stop?"

"Oh! Jesus Christ, no. Don't stop!"

"Are you sure? I will if you want me to."

"No, no," I gasped.

"Then I'd best continue, hadn't I."

The gripping became stronger. Then the release. I lay back, arms outstretched, now beyond coherent speech and consumed by brain-busting pleasure.

"I want you to come, Eddie."

All I could do was shake my head. She reached over me and as she did ran a flat wet tongue along my body. Then trailed her nails back down my skin as she straightened herself. Then began gripping and releasing me again.

"Oh! Someone liked that, didn't they!" She repeated it. Then a third time and I was gone wave after wave.

CHAPTER 37

I awoke with a start. My bedside clock read 3 a.m. Somewhere a car's clutch grated home. A dog barked. The sounds of Camden Town in the small hours. Maxine was propped against a pillow. She had a small blue china bowl of tiramisu and a spoon on her lap but was staring across the room as though inspecting a painting. I watched her for a few seconds and she became aware of me, pecked my cheek and asked if she'd woken me.

"No. I had a bad dream. That you'd found someone else and gone off to Spain with them."

"Just keep taking the pills, Sutton!"

"I was watching you. You looked disturbed. What were you thinking?"

"About us."

"Oh?"

"That it was a shame we didn't meet a few years ago. All that wasted time." She slid down beside me and I felt a wave of warmth. "Because I know one of life's secrets that's only taken me thirty-nine years to discover."

"Which is?"

"The world hasn't invented a better medicine for coping with life. Than two people truly in love with each other!"

"You're pretty clever, toots. D'you know that?"

"You're cleverer."

"How d'you work that out?"

"You had the good sense to allow yourself to fall in love when you knew it was the right thing to do." Those lips that you could just go on kissing for ever pulled back in a smile and then she winked. "We'll be all right, you and me, Eddie. I work in a casino. Did I ever mention that? I know about evaluating odds and risk. And I reckon you're a pretty good bet."

"I hope so."

"I've got the right man this time. One, to ruin my lipstick, not my mascara."

"I remember sitting with you that night in the bar of the Freemont. You said the reason I probably hadn't married was because I hadn't found the right woman. You were right. Well, I have now, toots!"

She ate some of the tiramisu and said, "We never got round to dessert."

"I wonder why!"

"Here." And she fed me a spoonful. "What do you think?"

"It's okay."

"Oh, just okay? That was made with love, baby." She took some and licked her lips. "You might be right. I think it needs something to bring out its fuller flavour." She pulled back the duvet, gathered up a dollop of it, put bowl and spoon on the bedside table and smeared her handful over my crotch then began licking it off.

Her tongue and the warmth of her mouth got me hard again.

"Well, well! Who'd have thought my tiramisu would have had such an effect on you."

"Miss Andrews?"

"Yes."

"Seems to me it would be a downright shame to let such a good erection go to waste."

"D'you know something, Mister Sutton. I couldn't agree with you more!"

I awoke at 7 a.m. The street lights were still on, but had no impact against the gathering light. Maxine stirred. Even in a T-shirt too big for her and hair in her eyes she looked sexy. She stretched then yawned. I asked her if she wanted a drink but she said 'no'. She was going home for some more sleep and a bath, then yawned again. She asked what kind of a day I had ahead. I wondered whether to tell her. Thought not. Then decided she'd be angry if she heard second hand.

"Jack and I are going to deliver the ransom."

She was up, eyes wide open. She hooked a finger in my T-shirt and pulled me closer.

"Do you have to go?"

"Yes."

"Let Jack and what's his name, Terry, do it. Why you?"

"I have to. It's all been set up."

"But why?"

"I have to."

"Be careful, Eddie. I still say Jack and Terry should go."

"Maxine!"

"Don't give me that 'a man's gotta do what a man's gotta do' crap, Sutton. This isn't Hollywood, and you're not John Wayne!"

"Then I won't!"

"Ring me when it's done."

"I will."

"Promise."

"I promise."

"Scout's honour!"

"Maxine!"

"Say it. I promise, scout's honour!"

"I promise, scout's honour."

"Now you have to. Or," she said, "kidnappers or not, you'll have me to contend with." She squeezed her soft female biceps and said, "Because I got muscles, Sutton. And don't you forget it!"

"As soon as it's done. I promise."

"Good. Very good." And she kissed me.

She gathered up her clothes strewn around the bedroom. Went into the bathroom and came out dressed. She'd shoved her hair around. And while it didn't look as respectable and groomed as when she was at work, it no longer looked the worse for two marathon sessions.

"You don't have to go, toots. You can stay here while I'm out. This place should be as much yours as it is mine."

She said it was sweet of me. But she was going. I slipped on a dressing gown and saw her to the front door.

"You will be careful, won't you?"

"No. I'm going there with a notice across my forehead 'Feel free to kill me!'"

"Don't be so bloody funny! Get used to someone caring about you."

"Sorry."

"Speak to you later. I'm not going to go on about it except to say if an opportunity occurs to get out of it, take it." She gave me a long hard kiss, then walked around the corner to her car.

I came back upstairs to the kitchen. Put my hand in the dressing gown pockets and felt a piece of paper in one of them. It was a scribbled note that read 'I love you'. I put the coffee on and noticed my notepad and pencil usually by the phone was on the table. I smiled, pulled a mug from the cupboard and found another note in it reading '*I love you lots*'. I made the coffee, lifted the sugar bowl lid. There was a third note, '*Lots and lots*'. *Signed anonymous.*

CHAPTER 38

I arrived at Liverpool Street Station just after 11 a.m. There were two entrances. One from Bishopsgate, carrying the main traffic where all the shops were, the other from Broadgate, where all the steel and glass high-rise office buildings were. The station concourse was huge, its perimeter demarcated by concessions. Snack joints, a pizza place, newsagents. And busy, very busy with a kaleidoscope of faces, colours, nationalities, waiting around, queueing at ATMs, on their phones, on the move, or standing looking at the huge electronic information board below a glass roof admitting long rays of autumn sunshine that poured onto us. There were others as well, just standing around cocking an ear to announcements about arrivals and departures from a tannoy that seemed never to run out of something to say. I looked at the faces. Recognised none. Then looked up to the first-floor gallery for Terry.

Platform 10 was about centre. I took up a position behind a pillar at 9. You could see the metal train departure information frames quite clearly. There were four individual glass-fronted boards about two foot by four foot, attached back to back and side to side with four others of the same size. The whole arrangement housed within a free standing tubular steel frame. They'd chosen the spot well, affording them two platform options to jump on trains if necessary or alternatively the use of the underground, which was close by, to take them to Christ knows where if required. Or if that wasn't enough, a thousand people to get lost among. I asked Terry through my mobile if he'd seen anything.

"Nothing!"

"Keep looking."

It was nearly noon. I checked for the umpteenth time that my disguise, beard and moustache, and steel-framed glasses, was still in place. A Network Rail steward in yellow luminous bib, frayed grey shirt and shiny navy trousers, asked if he could help.

"Just waiting for a friend. All right to stay here?"

"No problem!"

A male Japanese backpacker stopped by the frames, ran a finger down some detail and moved on. An Asian woman pushing a buggy looked at them for nearly a minute, and ambled off. A tall blonde, thin-lipped, cropped hair like straw, in jeans and white T-shirt with I AM A VIRGIN printed across its front walked past. As she did, I noticed in much smaller lettering on the back, the words THIS IS A VERY OLD T-SHIRT. The tannoy boomed above the noise. I tried to look everywhere at once. It was clear to me this wasn't the job for two blokes. One upstairs. The other disguised like a cross between the mad professor and Leon Trotsky. But a job for the police. They did this stuff so well. They were organised, co-ordinated, with however much manpower was needed. But this was how Jack had wanted it. So, that's what he'd got.

And then there he was coming down the stairs from the Bishopsgate entrance. Navy suit, white shirt, navy tie, carrying a black zip-up document case. He looked around, got his bearings. Spotted platform 10, then the train departure information frames and made his way to left luggage.

"I've just seen Jack," Terry was saying in my ear.

"I have him."

"There's a geezer just by the entrance in jeans, leather jacket, baseball cap and dark glasses. Could be the croupier what's his name?"

I tried looking but there were too many people in the way. Their patterns broke up then reformed but still prevented me from seeing him.

It took Jack about five or six minutes to leave the case at left luggage. He stood close to the end board as though looking for information, glanced left and right a couple of times then slid the white paper receipt in the gap between the front and rear boards, looked about again and walked off.

"I think it's Houston," Terry said. "He's definitely been clocking Jack. He's making his way amongst a crowd to your end."

I could just see him now, through a knot of people, standing around an ATM, collar up, cap down.

"Anyone watching him, Terry?"

"Two coppers strolling, doing the rounds. One's looked him over a couple of times. There's a blonde in sunglasses having a cup of something to your 3 o'clock. She's looked at him twice. Maybe she just fancies him 'cause she's now started reading a mag."

So who was Ricky working for? I asked myself. Because this wasn't something he could do alone. Well, I'd soon find out. Because the plan was to let him lift the book, then follow him. Or if he went back to his flat, beat the shit out of him until I got the truth.

Jack walked past me, hands in jacket pockets, towards the Broadgate exit. Houston began circling him, moving slowly but clearly towards the frames. I lost sight of him a couple of times behind knots of people. When he reappeared he was within thirty feet of the boards. He stopped, took off his cap and wiped his forehead. He looked my way. I took off my glasses and with hands covering my face, pretended to clean them with a tissue. He looked up at the gallery; something had caught his eye because he continued staring. Then he looked around the concourse. At me, then up at the gallery again. He stood there for a few seconds as if he was re-assuring himself about something and then he bolted.

"He's clocked me, Eddie! He's doing a runner."

"Get down here now and watch the receipt."

"What you gonna do?"

I was already doing it. Running through the crowds after him while ripping off my disguise.

"Get hold of the little shit and beat the fucking living daylights out of him until I get the truth!" I yelled.

CHAPTER 39

He took the stairs three at a time, barging people out of his way. Bishopsgate was clogged with pedestrians in the pleasant sunshine. Two cars jerked to a halt just avoiding colliding as Houston sprinted across the main road, passed a police station, and raced down Middlesex Street. I followed weaving my way between traffic. He was thirty yards ahead, the sides of his jacket flapping like wings. My lungs burned. I told myself that soon he'd run out of steam and I'd have him. But he didn't. He darted round a turning. By the time I got there he'd vanished. There were just grimy Victorian buildings and empty pavements. I doubled over hands on hips. It took a while to find a second wind. I tried several doors but they were locked. Then two pensioners came around the corner. I asked if they'd seen a man of Houston's description.

"I should say I have," said the women.
"Which way did he go?"
"Nearly sent me flying."
"Which way!"
"Into the market."

Wentworth Street market was just a morass of people. Black, nearly black, white, yellow and a din of voices. Every turn of my head bought a new colour to my eyes. The greens and reds of fruit and veg. Blues, white, pinks, greys of sweaters, jackets, hanging from stalls that all claimed the cheapest prices. Different smells permeated the air, burgers, pizzas, body odour, perfume. I edged my way through the crowd searching hundreds of faces for one particular one. But it wasn't there.

I came out of the market into Commercial Street and sat on a bus stop shelter seat for more breath. I decided to head for Aldgate East tube, because one stop would put me right back in the Liverpool Street station concourse and I was just too pooped to walk it. I dragged myself up and there he was further down across the road, hailing a cab that didn't stop. Another second and I would have been out of sight. But I didn't get it. He looked my way and was off again, towards the High Street with me now not that far behind.

He vaulted the pedestrian pavement guard to get across the road in one lithe flowing movement that I knew I couldn't emulate. As I got to it, a cold shiver went through me as a Rav4 jeep speeding round from the Mansell Street carriageway to join the main road first hooted then slammed on its brakes. Its wheels locked, screeching, the sound ascending above all other noises as it tried to make a harder purchase on the tarmac. Then they smoked and the smell of burning rubber filled the air. I could hear a voice a long way off which I recognised as mine yelling 'watch out'. He turned too late. His hands went out in front of him as though he could prevent the inevitable.

The Rav's bullbar crunched right into his ribs. He went up in the air and hung there for a moment like a twisted rag doll, then he hit the road, bounced and as he rolled cracked his skull against the wheel hub of a lorry parked at the kerb beneath a road safety advertising hoarding reading WATCH THE TRAFFIC FLASH PAST YOUR EYES. NOT YOUR LIFE. There were a few convulsive twitches. Then he lay there. Still. The Rav's drivers' door opened. A few seconds passed. Then a tall guy with a round face lurched out. I watched as he took a few steps towards the body then vomited down his shirt. He stood there looking, just looking, as bits of his last meal dripped onto the tarmac.

I ran to Ricky and crouched beside him. There was a deep gash across his forehead and one on his chin. Another at his temple bled so much the blood streamed down the side of his face and soaked into his collar. Conditioning made me seize the moment. I leaned right over as though putting an ear to his chest while my hand, shielded by my body, searched a couple of pockets. There was a wallet in one and a mobile in another. I slipped both into my own jacket.

People came out of shops. First-floor windows opened. In under a minute there was a crowd. An Asian guy from a supermarket opposite asked if there was anything he could do. A voice behind said it would ring for an ambulance. But looking at Ricky's bleeding twisted face I thought a priest more appropriate. The shopkeeper asked if I was all right. I was about to tell him to try and hold back the crowd when it split of its own accord and a small man in a serge suit and bifocals pushed through announcing he was a doctor.

He kept asking Ricky if he could hear him and what his name was. But there was no response. He put an ear to his chest. Then two fingers under Ricky's chin and tilted his head back, pinched his nose and began blowing into his mouth. But nothing happened. He lifted his eyelids back. Then started chest compressions. He was working hard. He kept compressing, then blowing, then compressing. The Asian guy asked if there was anything he could get from his shop. The doctor rolled back Ricky's eyelids again, shook his head and said 'no', because he was dead.

The crowd had grown larger. There were no police or paramedics yet to take control. Two women and a postman got alongside of me and were slowly edging me backwards. I let them and anyone else who wanted to.

Some workmen in donkey jackets and boots got themselves into the crowd and started shepherding it back. In the few minutes it took them to gain control, I'd worked my way to the periphery then simply walked away before anyone thought to ask about witnesses.

I went first to the information boards. But the receipt had gone. I was expecting to find Terry. He'd gone too. I found a bar upstairs and ordered a Scotch and downed half. I went through Ricky's wallet. Just credit cards and three twenty-pound notes. A picture of him hanging in the air went through my mind and though he'd only been there seconds, in my head it took him ages to drop and when he did the thud sent a shiver through me. I'd seen road traffic accidents in my time. But I didn't think I'd ever forget today's. It wasn't the blood. It was the look on his twisted face. I'm no doctor. But my guess was he'd broken his neck hitting the parked lorry. I downed the other half and ordered a refill and while the waiter was getting it, rang Terry. A voice, not his, asked who I was.

"More to the point, who are you? And why do you have my friend's mobile?"

"I'm a first aid officer. Your friend, Mister Cooper, was the subject of an attack!"

"Jesus! What happened?" I could hear Terry in the background asking for the phone. Then he was on the line. "You all right?" I asked.

"I'll live. I was watching you know what, when the blonde walked passed me and sprayed ammonia in my eyes. Then kneed me in the bollocks. I ended up on the floor. Someone called first aid and they brought me here."

I asked him where 'here' was. He asked the first aider, who told him it was at station reception, which was at platform 10, right beside the left luggage office, for a bit of irony.

I cancelled the drink and a couple of minutes later was in the first aid room. Which was more like a gigantic cupboard with space for just three. It had a large black PVC couch upon which Terry sat. A small wall cupboard with doors open showed all their paraphernalia, plasters, bandages, disinfectant.

"How is he?"

"I'm okay," said Terry, who lay pasty-faced, propped against the upright of the couch, with cotton wool pads over his eyes. "I ever get hold of that fucking bitch …" Then he remembered where he was.

"And the balls?"

"Seems like he's over the worst of that," said the officer, who was tall with a gut hanging over his trouser belt and looked as though if he didn't lose weight he might need a colleague's help one of these days.

"And the eyes?"

"I've washed them out with saline solution. But he should go to an A & E."

"Well?" Terry asked me.

"Gone. Never mind that for the moment."

He asked to have the pads removed. The officer protested then had to give in. Terry blinked. His eyes were puffy and bloodshot as if he'd been in a punch-up then stayed up all night. He waved his hand in front of his face, then got off the couch a little shakily and said he'd be all right.

"Go to your local A & E and get them checked out."

"Will do" and he thanked the man for all his help. He said he could do with a drink. Then asked what had happened.

I told him about Ricky.

"That'll teach him a lesson."

"He was a decoy, and I fell for it."

"Don't beat yourself up over it!" Which I thought was a

nice thing to say seeing as I should have been comforting him. "Presumably the bitch what done me took the receipt and claimed the book?"

"I would guess!"

"So what now?"

"Tony turns up in a cab. Or gets thrown out of a car somewhere."

We sat in the bar. I had a single. Terry a double.

"You rung Jack?"

"Not yet."

Terry thought for a moment and said,

"Don't. We'll go back to the house. If Tony's there, all this won't matter. If he isn't, it'll be better coming from us face to face."

"Okay. But give me a minute. I've got a phone call to make."

"Go on, then. I haven't finished with this place yet." He clicked his fingers at a passing waiter and ordered another double. "Eddie?" I shook my head.

I pulled out a mobile. Ricky's. Was about to use my own and thought, what the hell. I knew Maxine's number off by heart. But I went through his contacts before dialling. There was Tony, Zoe, Lenny, and about a dozen others including Maxine's. I pressed 'call' and she answered.

"Ricky?"

"It's Eddie."

"Baby, I've been so worried. What happened? Are you okay?"

"I'm fine." There was a pause and she said,

"Why are you using Ricky Houston's phone?"

"Why does he have your number, Maxine?"

"Why? All the staff do. In case of an emergency. What happened, baby; are you okay?"

I told her about him being a decoy and the accident.

"Shit! But you're okay?"

"Yes."

"What about delivering you know what?"

"It's done."

"So when does boy wonder appear?"

"Your guess is as good as mine. What is your guess?"

"How the hell would I know! And what the hell is that supposed to mean? What's going on, Eddie?"

"Nothing!"

"You sound as though you're about to lose your temper. D'you have beef with me over something?"

"Should I?"

"Don't play games with me, Eddie. I don't like it. If there's something wrong, or you've got something to say, have the balls to say it!"

"In a minute. I'll ring you back." I clicked the phone and tapped it against my chin. There was something wrong all right. There had been from the start. It was staring me in the face. But I couldn't see it.

CHAPTER 40

I went back to Terry who'd nearly finished his drink. He asked who I'd phoned and I told him Maxine.

"Ah! The lovely Maxine."

"D'you know if Jack went into any further details with her other than Tony being kidnapped? Like the ransom? Or the delivery?"

He rocked the last drop of his drink as if he couldn't make up his mind about another and said,

"Shouldn't think so. Why? Hey, you don't think …?"

I picked up the bill. Terry said he'd get it. But I told him it was on me. Besides if he'd seen what they were charging for a single and two doubles, he'd probably have needed more eye drops. I thought about Ricky having Maxine's number as I waited for my change. For emergencies, she'd said. Perfectly plausible. I wondered if she'd ever contacted him. Why would she need to? She wouldn't! I looked at his phone in front of me, knowing what had to be done wanting to know if there was a message on it from her to him. But why would there be if it only got used for emergencies? Her sister's connection with Spain had always been on my mind even though it had been explained. And it occurred to me that I'd never actually checked the story out. Or ever got back to Stafford with her DOB. I told myself she wasn't involved. If he had her number for emergencies only, there was no reason for her to ring him. So if I checked his messages, there shouldn't be any from her, should there? I lifted the phone, then put it back on the table. I sat there looking at it for the aggro it might hold that I might not know how to deal with. 'You're just being a copper, Sutton,' a voice in my head said. I lifted the phone and put it down again. Lifted it again, and put it down again. Then lifted it and pressed the on button, then turned it off. What if there was a message from her to Ricky? What then? I sat there staring at it, afraid of what I might hear. But in the end a man's gotta do what a man's gotta do. Isn't that what they say? I clicked and waited. He'd had two messages. Both left that day. The first from a girl called Sharon about a party they'd been invited to in Wandsworth. My guts knotted as I waited for the second. I was tempted to cancel it out. But knew I couldn't. I had to hear it. Good or bad. I had to know if the good guys were really bad guys! The second message was also from a girl. Her name was Zoe. "Got the book from left luggage! Going home. Then on to Tony, to spend the night with him. Ring me."

The waiter had the change on a silver-coloured platter. All I could do was stare at it because I was saying a silent prayer to Jesus and I've not prayed since I was a kid.

"Sir. You gave me a twenty. That's the change. Is there a problem?"

"What? Yes. What? No, here," and I tipped him.

I told Terry there had been a change of plan. I was going to put him in a cab back to Jack, because there was an errand I had to run.

"You lost your bottle about facing him?"

"No. Just tell him I found the last piece of the jigsaw." I walked him through the concourse and up the stairs out to Bishopsgate. It was still sunny. He was still limping. I put him in a taxi, then walked around the corner to my car. I sat there for a moment realising what an idiot I'd been. Talk about missing the obvious.

I rang Maxine. She said 'hello'.

"It's 2.30 p.m."

"So?"

"I thought it was high time someone told you that they loved you today."

"Do you?"

"Yes."

"You over whatever it was on your mind?"

"Yes."

"Was it to do with us?"

"No. It was to do with me being as thick as two short planks!"

"Is that true?

"Absolutely!"

"I thought for a moment I was going to get a Dear Maxine."

"Don't even think it. Because it could never happen."

"I believe you."

"Do you?"

"Yes."

"Scout's honour?"

"Ha, ha!" she laughed.

"Say it."

"I believe you. Scout's honour!"

"Good. Because it's true."

"I believe you. I love you, Eddie! Your problem is, dopey, you've just no idea how much. Are you coming up to the Freemont this evening?"

"Yes."

"Good. Very good. I have a break about 8 p.m.-ish. I want to buy us a meal to celebrate."

"Celebrate what?"

"Two people who in this lunatic world found each other."

A lump came up in my throat, and it took me a while to get hold of what I wanted to say.

"Eddie?"

"Maybe I could sit across the table from you. Hold your hand in my hands and tell you how much I love you, and how much you mean to me."

"Eddie Sutton!"

"What!"

"You fraud! You're really just an old romantic underneath all that macho!"

"Don't tell anyone!"

"Want to know a secret?"

"Go on."

"If you promise to be as naughty a boy tonight as you were last night, I might just let you hold both my hands!"

"Sounds like an offer I can't refuse!"

CHAPTER 41

I buzzed a couple of times. But there was no answer. I opened the street-door and her flat-door locks with a lock pick and a fifteen-inch square of plastic. Not hard if you know what you're doing. I sat waiting in her bedroom. Her smell, the sharp expensive scent of Dior hung in the room, on the bed and throughout the flat. The day was turning dusk. A draught whistled from the window in the near darkness. My watch read 4pm I wondered if she'd been and gone. But she hadn't because her car was parked outside. I looked across the room at the bed and thought I should have put it together long before this. It was me thinking she was lying about knowing Leon that had given me myopia.

Her key clicked in the latch and the door slammed. She walked in and a shaft of light from the hall silhouetted her momentarily in the rectangle of the doorway. She turned on the light and clutching a hand to her breasts nearly jumped backwards through the door she'd come through.
"Jesus Christ! You nearly frightened the life out of me! What the hell are you doing here?"
"Waiting for you, Zoe."
"How d'you get in, Colombo? Silly question, I suppose," she said, throwing her jacket and shoulder bag on the bed. She put her hands on her hips, her face a picture of anger. "So what d'you want? Whatever it is, make it quick. I'm in a hurry!"
"Going on a date?"

"And if I was? I know I said we'd get together. But not tonight."

"Tony's welcome to you."

She asked what I meant by that. I threw Ricky's phone across to her. She made no attempt to catch it. Just let it bounce on the double bed and fall on the carpet.

"That's Ricky's. I picked up your message."

"Sorry. You've lost me."

"Where's Tony?"

She stepped across the room to the walk-in wardrobe, brushing her legs and skirt against my knees.

"Eddie, baby! You were paid to find him. Remember?"

"Don't piss me around, Zoe. It's over."

"You must have picked up an old message." She turned. Her face had a quizzical expression. "How come you've got his phone?"

"Because he's dead. I took it off his body."

"Yeah, right! Now who's been watching too much television!"

I explained about the accident after he'd played decoy while she lifted the book. The colour drained from her face. She bit her lip.

"I've no idea what you're talking about." She said.

"How does this sound? Danny was blackmailing Tony."

She shrugged nonchalantly and said,

"I told you that."

"Then one day Jack mentions to Tony Ronnie's died and he's been left a bequest. He either mentioned Ronnie's insurance. Or Ronnie told Tony about what he had when they were dealing in Jack's absence."

She shrugged again and said, "So?"

"So with the book Tony would be able to blackmail Carlin. No more worries about the debt . Maybe even get Carlin sent down. But how to get it? Jack's not going to give it to him because it's going to be locked in a safe in Hampstead. Or more likely a safety-deposit box in town. So he dreamed up this kidnap caper with the book as ransom."

"Walt Disney should have had your imagination, Colombo!"

"But he needed accomplices. That's you and Ricky. You're up for it because of Tony. And Ricky's up for it because it gives him access to Danny's drug connections and pays Danny back for stealing Davina. Two birds with one book! Your first problem though was Jack hired me. So you tried pumping me for information using your bed. But then you've got form for that kind of stuff going right back to 2008, haven't you?"

"You fucking bastard!"

"You must really love him. But how much can he love you letting you do it? The fictitious letter as bait to get me over was a good touch. I'll give you that. The other problem about Jack hiring me was that Tony couldn't be sure I hadn't equipment for combing out telephone voice distortions or knew someone who had. Hence the ransom note. Was it you or Ricky that spiked it on the car?" She didn't reply, just kept looking, keeping a blank expression. "My guess is you, once we were all inside the prayer hall. Not that it matters now!"

The corner of her bottom lip began twitching. She wiped it with a thumb to stop it, and I knew I'd guessed right.

"The second mistake was underestimating Danny. He wasn't going to give up so easily recovering the CD. Lenny Jordan died in- directly because of it. And Collette killed a friend of mine because she thought he knew about it. Danny's not a nice person, and way above your league. And talking of murder. You do know your Tony killed Davina? I thought it was because she set him up. But he mistook something she said on the phone in her office about what she'd come back from Spain with. Not the book, but her father's property."

"Rubbish! My Tony wouldn't have done that."

"The next time he loses his temper with you, you may end up with more than just a kicking."

"You don't know my Tony like I do. He wouldn't have done that."

"Wake up, Zoe! Or are you stupid as well as poisonous? He's just using you. Like you tried to use me."

I picked up her bag, brown leather and expensive looking, and rummaged through it.

"Hey!" she exclaimed, trying to snatch it back.

I grabbed hold of a fistful of her shirt, pulled her towards me then shoved her so hard against the wardrobe she bounced off the door. There was a blonde wig, sunglasses, purse, mobile, but no book.

"Well, well!" I said, pointing to the wig. I went through her jacket and took a bunch of keys from a pocket. "So. Let's see. You haven't come in with the book. You haven't been to Tony yet. You've put it in your car on the way in, right? So all that remains is for you to tell me where Tony's holed up."

"Go fuck yourself!"

"You got two choices."

"Really?"

"Tell me and maybe Jack can fix things. Maybe. Or I'll tell Danny about lover boy killing Davina. And in the not too distant future, Tony will end up hanging by his ankles from a beam as Collette cuts his testicles off, one at a time."

She gagged at the imagery then said,

"Like you would."

"Oh, I would! In the last few days I've been threatened, roughed up and had my head nearly cracked open with a brick and almost run down by a car trying to kill me which I dare say was driven by Tony. I've had your drug-dealing, wanna-be Al Capone boyfriend up to here. I've already had money off Jack. So it's all in a day's work as far as I'm concerned. Besides, he's got it coming. Because all drug dealers do, regardless of who their parents are. And so do you!"

"What does that mean?"

"Once Danny knows about your involvement, he'll hand you over to Collette as her Christmas bonus. She won't be after information this time. It'll be just the sheer pleasure of hurting you, while her girlfriend films it all. Stroke, after stroke, after stroke, with that cane while her nipples get harder and harder. No stopping, until she either gets bored. Or comes from the excitement."

"You bastard! You fucking bastard!"

"You better believe it. Because it's about time you paid your dues in this affair! So, Zoe, as I'm sure as so many times before, Tony's testicles are in your hands!"

"You're a real fucking comedian, aren't you! He's three times the man you are, Sutton. And good for it three times a night. Not like some clapped-out forty-year-old."

"Clapped out forty-year old eh! So all your heavy breathing and gasping the other afternoon was down to an asthma attack, was it?"

"Go to hell!"

"And talking of Collette. When she finds out you're an actress and she will, I guarantee it. She'll cut your face for spite, because that would really give her a kick. Try getting an acting job after that."

Zoe ran the back of her hand along her jaw, looked away and said,

"Flat 3, Laurel Court, 1690 Hammersmith Broadway."

CHAPTER 42

I shoved her in the wardrobe and stuck a chair under the handle so quickly she hadn't any time to realise what had happened. She began shouting and swearing, then banging on the door. I picked up Ricky's phone and rang Jack.

"Where the hell have you been?" He screamed. "I've been ringing and ringing you!"

"Sorry. Lost my mobile," I lied. "Where are you?"

"At the Freemont. Never mind that. Where's Tony?" he yelled. "Terry told me what happened. Where's my son!"

"He's safe."

"How d'you know? Where the hell is he, Sutton! Where!"

I told him it was complicated and that I needed to speak to him. But he kept demanding to know where Tony was. I told him the police were probably bugging his line so unless he wanted them to get to Tony first, he should wait until I got to the club. He calmed down a bit and asked what all the banging and shouting in the background was about.

"That's Zoe effing and blinding."

"Why?"

"I can't tell you."

"Just get over here, Eddie."

"Where's Terry?"

"At the house. Lying on a bed with eye pads on."

"Tell him to get over to Zoe's with some rope or handcuffs if he has any."

"Why?"

"I can't tell you. You'll have her address at the club."

"You sure my Tony's safe?"

"Positive. Oh, and Jack, have the rest of my money ready. Because when I tell you my little tale, you'll know I'm done with this business!"

Zoe was still kicking the door. But it was strong and wasn't going to give.

"Open this fucking door, Sutton!" she shrieked. "Never mind Tony losing his balls. I'll cut yours off personally!"

Twenty minutes later I buzzed Terry into the flat. His eyes were still bloodshot. But the puffiness was subsiding and he seemed quite bright seeing what he'd been through.

"So what's going on?" he asked.

"I want you to babysit Zoe while I go to Jack. She's not to be out of your sight. She's not to make any calls. D'you bring some rope with you?"

"These." And he waved a pair of handcuffs in front of me.

We went into the bedroom. She was still swearing and kicking.

"What's her problem?"

"She wants to get out so she can warn Tony to leave the flat he's holed up in."

"I thought he'd been kidnapped."

"So did I. Don't worry. Jack'll explain everything later. Oh, by the way," I said, pointing to the wig and sunglasses on the bed, "she's the one that sprayed you with ammonia."

He picked up the wig and ran the hair through his fingers.

"Really!"

"Yeah. You ready?" I pulled the chair away and stepped aside. The door burst open and she slammed right into him.

"Not so fast," he said shoving her so hard against a wall she winced and rubbed her arm.

"That was assault, Quasimodo!" she screamed. "I could have the law on you. You could end up in prison. Or a zoo."

He hit her without warning, his palm across her face and before her cheek blanched hit again with the back of his hand.

"No. *That* was assault!"

She staggered backwards. Tried to grab the chair, missed and ended up on her backside. He dragged her across the room by her shirt collar and secured her wrists around the central heating pipes with the handcuffs. Then stood over her and said,

"You give me any trouble, I'll beat the shit out of you. Understand?"

"I need to go to the bathroom."

"Do it on the carpet."

I told him to keep her there until I rang. Then uncuff her and let her go.

"Not before I've given her a good slapping, put her on the bed, pulled her knickers down and shown her my balls are okay."

She pulled at the pipes. But they wouldn't give. She suddenly looked quite frightened, the bravado all gone.

The book was in a plastic bag under the spare tyre. I swung by my place, picked up the CD so that I had the full set for Jack. I wondered how to start to tell him his son was rubbish. I rehearsed a few openings. But nothing seemed right.

CHAPTER 43

He asked where Tony was without even a 'hello'. I told him to sit down.

"He's, he's, not …?"

"No. Nothing like that."

"Thank goodness! So?"

"I don't know how to say this, Jack. So right out is the best way."

"What d'you mean?"

"There never was a kidnapping."

He looked confused. His brow knitted, his eyes narrowed almost hidden under his eyebrows. He looked as he had at the cemetery after finding the letter. Trying to understand the incomprehensible.

"What d'you mean?"

I explained about Danny. The drug dealing. The blackmailing of Tony over fiddling the casino. And that Tony was going to use the book to turn the tables on Carlin. I dropped into a chair and said, "Sorry." It seemed such an ineffectual thing to say. But it was all I could think of.

Jack just stood there, transfixed, shaking his head from side to side, side to side.

"No, you got it wrong, Eddie! My Tony wouldn't do that," he said at last. "Not my Tony."

"'Fraid so Jack. I have the CD of Danny organising Tony so his people could fiddle your tables."

He slumped into a chair, looking at me as if he didn't who I was.

"Jesus Christ!" he exclaimed. Then he asked where he was now.

"Flat 3, Laurel Court, 1690 Hammersmith Broadway."

He lifted a phone and said he wanted to speak to Kevin, gave him the address, and told him he wanted him and a couple of his crew, who knew how to keep their mouths shut, to go to the flat, get Tony and take him to Jack's house.

"Don't let him out of your sight until I get there. Or make any phone calls. Oh and Kevin," he added, "you have my permission to kick in whatever doors are necessary!"

"That was the good news, Jack. Now for the bad." He looked wan and absolutely deflated as though he'd just put on ten years in the last few minutes. "Tony killed Davina!"

"No. No, no, no! That I don't believe. No, that I just won't have."

I told him probably not on purpose. But that was how it was. Not, as I had thought, because she'd set him up with Danny. But because he believed she had Ronnie's book.

"The cops have CCTV of his car near her flat. They have his image on the video entryphone. Arresting and charging him will entitle them to take a DNA swab. My guess is it'll match DNA on Davina's face."

He put his head in his hands.

"How could all this have happened? He has everything. Everything!"

I didn't say anything. Because sometimes you just know to keep your gob shut.

He finally looked up and asked,

"What should I do?"

I'd bluffed Zoe about handing over Tony to Carlin. But I really didn't care what happened to him. Because drug dealers deserve all they get.

"What should I do, Eddie? Please help me here. You're

an ex-copper."

He suddenly looked quite sad and pathetic. And I got to thinking. All this misery and none of it his fault.

"I can only tell you what I'd do in your place, Jack."

"Which is?"

"Sooner or later the cops will pick Tony up. So be pro-active. Go with him and a solicitor ... D'you know a good one?"

"Stan Markham. I've known him for over twenty years. He's the best."

"All three of you go to Kensington nick and Tony tells the cops he understands the police want to speak to him and he's voluntarily attending to see how he's able to help them. And when Stafford interviews him, which this Markham guy will insist is in his presence, you'll know precisely what the law have got in evidence. Then leave it to the brief."

"Is there an alternative?"

"Get him out of the country. But all ports and airports have been alerted. And if he gets out, which he won't, he'll never be able to come back. That's if he's not found and extradited."

"Some choices."

"You asked. And I don't want to know what you plan. Because I don't want to be an accessory."

"That's fair enough!"

He closed his eyes and slumped back in the chair.

"The truth is I have no plan. This has happened too quickly. I need to think. I need to make a few phone calls. I need to meet with a couple of people."

He said he had no plan. But I could feel there were ideas swimming around in his head.

"Where's the book I left at Liverpool Street?"

"In my car with the CD."

"I want it, please."

"Sure. I'll go and get it."

"He had everything. Why would he do this? He must have known I'd copy the stuff."

I told him it wouldn't have mattered. Because he'd have had what he needed to get Danny banged up. Even take over his drug business financed by blackmailing Leon.

He looked at me, his eyes brimming, his face white, haggard and said,

"What an idiot! What an idiot! Didn't he realise?"

"Realise what?"

"That sooner or later someone would have killed him! Was Maxine in on this?"

"Absolutely not."

"Good. She's becoming very dear to me. What about the Zoe girlfriend?"

"Oh, yeah! Up to her neck. She's the one that lifted the book at the station."

"And his pal, Ricky?"

I thought he'd had enough for one evening. So I said 'yes'. But didn't go into any further details. It could wait.

"I'll get the stuff for you."

"Here!" He opened a drawer and tossed a small brown jiffy bag across his desk. "Your money. I'd like to think I can count on your silence."

"About what?"

"Thank you."

"What do I tell Maxine?"

"Leave that to me," he replied.

"I don't know how you're going to keep a lid on this, Jack, given the cops, Tony, Davina, Carlin."

"Neither do I. For the moment," he said, biting a thumbnail, "but I'll think of something. I'm sorry I got you into all this, Eddie."

"You weren't to know. Get yourself a cup of coffee. Or something stronger. I won't be long."

CHAPTER 44

I went in to Maxine. She kissed me then asked how I was and I told her 'fine'.

"Good. Is Tony back?"

"No. Jack wants to speak to you."

"He's not dead, is he?"

"No."

"Sounds serious though. What's up?"

"It's not good. He wants to tell you."

She took my arm and said,

"I told the chef to make the best tiramisu in the history of desserts because it's for my bloke."

"I don't think we should have a meal here tonight. It wouldn't be right, the way Jack is. The way things are. Maybe we could just have a coffee and a sandwich somewhere."

She looked disappointed then said,

"Okay, toots! If that's what you think."

"There's nothing to stop me telling you how much I love you over a sandwich."

She kissed her finger and touched my lips with it.

"I'll hold you to that, Sutton. Because I like you telling me how much you love me."

"Then afterwards go and see Jack. There's nothing you can do. Just tell him you're there for him."

She put the finger under my chin. We were eyeball to eyeball.

"Eddie. How serious?"

"Tony killed Davina."

"Jesus Christ! Are you sure?"

"Yes. And he fabricated his own kidnapping so he could use the ransom, which was an incriminating notebook of Ronnie's, to blackmail a few low lives who were fiddling the tables here."

She slumped into one of the chairs and held her hands momentarily over her face.

"I can't believe it. The kidnap thing I wouldn't put past him. But murder?"

"Manslaughter. I don't think he set out to kill her. I think his temper got the better of him."

"Even so! And what do you mean about fiddling the tables?"

"Let Jack explain it all. Just pretend you don't know what's happened. Okay? Don't tell him I told you anything, because I said I wouldn't. Okay?"

"Sure."

"I've got some stuff in the car for him. Then I'll see you by the bar. Ten minutes?"

"Okay, toots!"

I went downstairs to the car park. Rollers, Jags, Mercs nicely parked in respective whitewashed marked-out bays, gleaming under several security lights that bleached bits of the night. I took the stuff from the glove compartment, put it in my pocket and was heading back when I saw her. She was in a dark maroon cocktail dress with a single strand of pearls. She was slimmer than I remembered her. Her red hair was the same though, combed back, secured in a French pleat. She was leaning against a Jag so busy on her mobile that she didn't notice me.

I looked around. We were alone. There was one CCTV camera trained on the cars. But I really didn't care. The evening had turned windy and slightly chilly. You could just hear the traffic along Brompton Road.

"Ricky!" she was saying. "Where are you? It's 7.15 p.m.

Ring me back at once! You hear me, at once!"

"You won't be playing the tables tonight, Collette. He's not coming. On account of being dead." And then I hit her with the best left hook I've ever thrown. Even better than the one that laid out Joey Farmer. Something went crack. I thought for a second her jaw. But it was teeth and she spat some out. Blood began running down her chin onto her dress and soaked into it, just distinguishable against the dark maroon material. Then I kicked her in the shin with a nice deep blood-producing connection and as she bent over to tend it, I grabbed a fistful of her hair and slammed her head into the car window. Then once again, for luck. I hoped it would splinter and wreck her face. Unfortunately Jags are so good the glass held. Nevertheless, I knew I'd done her quite a bit of damage.

"That's for Arnie! And all the other poor sods you've had through your lock-up."

"I'll kill you for this, you bastard!" she shrieked over and over. She touched her mouth, saw the blood then spat out another couple of teeth. "I'll kill you!"

"Really!" So I kicked her hard again right in the shin wound and she crumpled. I went back into the club. I thought about ringing for an ambulance from one of the public telephones. Then thought, fuck it! Let the bitch bleed!

CHAPTER 45

Jack was behind his desk looking at the screens. But not taking anything in. A cup of coffee beside him had gone cold; the cream had congealed and lay like scum on the surface. He looked up as I closed the door and said,

"I still don't understand how all of this could happen. He has everything. It must be my fault. And yet Lucy with her boyfriend in Manchester ... I just don't understand ..."

I put the stuff on his desk.

"Don't listen to the CD tonight, Jack. You're too upset. Tomorrow."

He nodded. I wasn't sure he understood me. So I repeated myself.

"Yes, tomorrow. That's when I'll listen to it. Tomorrow. Are there copies?"

"If you mean me, absolutely not. You have my word on it. Maxine and I were going to grab a coffee and sandwich, unless you want her in here first. In which case, the food can wait."

"No, that's fine. It'll give me a chance to put the stuff away. How are you two doing?"

"We're good. Really good."

"That's nice."

Maxine was waiting by the bar and asked how Jack was. And I told her coming apart.

"Poor man. You were right about the meal, Eddie. It was very thoughtful. Maybe I should go up now."

"No, he said he was all right with us eating first."

"Okay. We can have our snack over there from bar service," she said, pointing to a large alcove with tables and chairs. "Then I'll go straight up and see him." We started walking over to it when she said, "Oh, I nearly forgot. Here. I bought you a present." She pulled a key ring from her pocket from which hung a mortice and two Yales. "To my flat."

"To what do I owe the honour?"

"I have plans for us."

"You mean tonight?"

"I was thinking more in terms of for ever!"

"Well, there's nothing like planning a little ahead, I suppose."

We were near the chairs when someone stepped in front of me. It took me a moment to register it was Collette, because she looked like a gargoyle with blood around her mouth as though she'd gone berserk with lipstick. She held a knife in her bloodstained hand; the blade caught the light of a chandelier as she thrust it at me. I raised an arm to defend myself and bang hers away. There was a scream. But not from her. I suspected from a customer, alarmed at what was happening. Then there was blood on my jacket. Just spots and blobs.

Suddenly Collette wasn't smiling. Her jaw dropped and I was momentarily amused by her mouth of missing teeth. Then something made me follow her line of sight. Maxine was holding her chest. There was blood spurting between her fingers. Her face was white, her lips losing colour. She looked at her chest, then at me and collapsed, as Collette bolted for the exit. I stood there looking for a couple of seconds, then reality crashed in. I shouted for someone to ring for an ambulance. People stood not moving for a moment and then three dialled at the same time.

"Tell 999 there's been a stabbing, possibly through the

heart!" I screamed.

People started moving. Two waiters yanked a table and chairs away so I could lay her flat. Another waiter brought towels and said, "Here, quick." I compressed the wound. But there was more blood now on her shirt, skirt, legs. Not gushing. But enough to alarm. I pressed down a little harder.

"Keep your eyes open, darling. Stay with me. What's your name? Tell me your name. Come on. It's such a pretty name. Tell me what it is." Parts of the white towels turned red. So I pressed harder. "Where's the ambulance!" I screamed. And then I heard Maxine saying something. Her voice low, almost a whisper.

"We'd have been good, me and you, Eddie. What a shame! Hold my hand. Don't let me die without you."

"No one's going to die, dopey! The ambulance will be here in seconds. Just try to stay conscious."

"Hold my hand." I did and she closed her eyes.

It had been six or seven minutes since the call. Then I heard sirens. They stopped and in a moment two uniformed PCs and a uniformed Inspector were looking at Maxine, then me. I look at them and then for the paramedics. More sirens and they were there, beckoned in by the police. Two of them, a man and a woman in their twenties, in yellow jackets, green shirts and dark trousers. And they were right on the case. The man called for something to raise Maxine's legs on and a waiter brought a stack of tablecloths. The female paramedic checked Maxine's airways, popped a mask over her nose and started squeezing a small bag attached to it. I told myself they wouldn't be doing all this if it was a lost cause. The man started chest compressions. He asked how long ago it had happened. I said maybe six or seven minutes.

Maxine's face was so white it struck me it looked as though she'd been embalmed and the simile was so painful I physically shook the thought from my head and filled it with memories of us. The meal at my place. Me telling her I loved her. The first real kiss after she told me she'd checked me out on Ubex. Her bouncing on my bed telling me we'd have to sell it and how much she loved me.

And then there was a doctor there in orange jumpsuit carrying a bag. He asked the girl about the condition. She told him. They exchanged a second look, but said nothing. It was a nothing that said everything and I went completely cold. He took over the compressions, put an ear to Maxine's chest, told the male paramedic to continue the compressions. In seconds he had a mobile defibrillator out and told both to stand back. I was reminded of TV hospital soaps and documentaries and how amused I got at the over-the-top drama when they do that. Not so funny now! He applied the paddles. Her body jumped. But there was no heart rhythm. He tried again. Nothing. He charged to 360. Still nothing. He tried again and again and again, a drop of sweat ran down his forehead and disappeared into his thin blond eyebrows. Her body jolted but there was no heart activity. He rolled back her eyelids and said he was calling it.

"No!" I screamed. "No. You can't. Try again. Please, please, please try again!" I was so beside myself with panic and anxiety and dread I was tempted to take the paddles from him. He tried again twice. Nothing. A third time. Still no rhythm. I kept imploring him to keep trying. And he did. But there was still nothing. He rolled back her eyelids again and said,

"I'm so dreadfully sorry." Then looked at the paramedics and said, "Death at 7.39 p.m." and the defibrillator was turned off.

I wanted to hold her in my arms. Cradle her and tell her it was all my fault. But I was prevented from touching her by a policeman. Someone found me a chair. I just sat, arms folded across my stomach, rocking back and forth, back and forth as my guts twisted up inside me. My temples began pounding. My mouth was so dry I could hardly swallow. I looked over at her lying there, eyes closed, motionless, thinking how important she was to me. How she'd become a dimension of my life and how I hadn't even had a chance to say goodbye. I started shaking from the pain which I knew would take years if ever to leave me.

At some point I became aware of things happening around me. CID were there and a murder squad. A PC took names and addresses. Someone quarantined the area with blue-and-white tape. Another uniformed told me I would have to accompany him to the station as I was a material witness. I told him later. He said now. I could tell he was trying to be kind and sensitive. But it was clear that he was going to take me, even if he had to put me under arrest. I reckoned it meant a couple of hours before I could be with her body. Someone tied plastic bags around my wrists to preserve the forensics. I kept telling myself it was all my fault. If I'd just left that mad bitch to her phone call and not hit her, none of this would have happened. If only I could turn the clock back thirty minutes. As I left, I looked over my shoulder at Maxine lying there, eyes closed, blood still damp on her clothes and swore to her I'd avenge her death by making everyone pay for this. Carlin, Doorrell, Tony, Zoe. But most of all, Collette. I'd spill everything to Stafford, every single thing I could remember about the book, the videos, everything. They would all pay for my Maxine's death. But it didn't help the pain.

I came out of the Freemont and walked towards the police car. The cold night air sent a shiver through me. And it must have been the wind blowing in my face because as I slid into the back seat, my eyes began brimming with tears.

Printed in Great Britain
by Amazon